A SLICE OF MYSTERY

SOPHIE MADDON

1

From: Lynn.James@RG.com

To: Abigail.Palmer@RG.com

Subject: Meeting

Meeting room 1 at 5pm.

Lynn, the project manager—also known as 'my boss' for the duration of this project—wanted to see me. The full stop indicated it wasn't anything good.

Ever since I was a little girl, I really wanted to be Sherlock Holmes. At least, ever since I read the novels, and saw the movies, and watched the TV shows. But a few things got in the way of my dream, parental expectations for one, and small details such as me not being a man, nor born in the nineteenth century. Details.

So, I did a business degree, joined R&G, a consultancy firm, straight out of uni, and went from project to project, commuting by car, train, and plane, generally not having much of a life or a laugh. But enough rambling.

I'd read and re-read Lynn's email twenty times, trying to glean clues, but had come up empty. I had to be honest, I wasn't sure Sherlock Holmes himself, master of deduction, could have done much better. The email was only five words long after all.

And now, five to five, I was walking to the room with my heart in my stomach. What if she was going to tell me I couldn't hack it on this project, and that I was fired from it, and that my future at the consultancy was under review? I didn't have much in term of savings, and moving back in with my parents was not an option.

No way.

I'd rather live in a flatshare with six other people than have to move back in with them. They were in France anyway, retired there a few years ago. My mum wanted a warmer climate, and my dad went along for the ride.

Lynn was already in the meeting room, looking even more sullen than usual. I didn't know if I'd ever seen her face not looking sour. Maybe it was just her face. I'd been told I constantly looked angry. I'd told these people it was genetics, not anger.

"What's wrong?" I asked immediately.

"Nothing," she said, but the slight tremor in her hands and voice told a different story.

If she didn't want to talk, I wouldn't make her, but curiosity was killing me. I sat down, glad she'd picked this room over those that had the hard-plastic chairs that made my butt fall asleep in two seconds flat.

"Abigail . . . I've had complaints about you," Lynn said.

I froze. Complaints were never good, especially if it had been the client complaining to Lynn. Those could get you kicked off a project faster than you could say Moriarty. I wondered what the complaint was about. I'd butted heads with a few people this week. I was one of the top experts in my field, that wasn't bragging, that was just the way it was, so yes, I did know better than the client how to setup their future system, and I wasn't going to let a condescending arrogant ass, who'd looked at the system for all of five minutes, tell me I was doing it wrong.

"Abigail?" Lynn's tone made me realise my mind had wandered.

"Sorry, I heard you. You said you'd received a complaint?"

"Not *a* complaint. Complaints. Plural."

I didn't know what to say to that. The fact that people complained about me didn't bother me per se. In my opinion, it meant I was doing something right. I was more worried about the impact on my ability to pay my heating bills this winter.

"People are complaining, among other things, about your nosiness, specifically that you keep on inserting yourself in conversations that aren't any of your business."

My eyes widened and a small cauldron of anger bubbled in my stomach. "Who said that?"

"That was Gemma, when you literally stepped into her meeting and told her, in front of the client, that the way she wanted to set up suppliers in the system was wrong."

"But it *was* wrong, and I was right!"

"Maybe you were, but that's beside the point. What were you doing barging in a meeting you were not invited to? What were you doing telling her she was wrong? You know how we handle these things Abigail, you've been with R&G for a decade, how can you do this?"

I pressed my lips together so hard I could almost taste blood. She had a point. One of the cardinal rules of consulting was the same as for divorced parents. You didn't disagree or fight in front of the kids, or in this case, the client. Nothing I could say now would make it better, so I stayed silent, observing her.

"That's not why you asked me to come here," I said after a minute.

She looked wrong-footed. Point for me. I always got a happy tingle when I applied Sherlock Holmes' techniques and got it right.

"How do you know?" she asked, her voice shaking a little.

I shrugged. "If the complaints were the reason you'd called me in here, then there should have been a relief of tension once you'd told me. But you telling me changed nothing. You didn't get less nervous, the 'oh it's over' thing, and you didn't get more nervous. Or is it nervouser? Either way. If you had been worried about my reaction, you would have gotten more nervous, but you didn't. So I have to assume that the complaints have nothing to do with why I'm here."

Colour drained out of Lynn's face and she looked taken aback. Everybody did, when I did what Hannah called my parlour trick. She'd get a kick out of hearing about this one.

"I'm impressed," Lynn said, and some colour returned to her ashy skin. "People in the office told me you were a Sherlock Holmes disciple—"

"Really?" I interrupted. "They used the word 'disciple?'"

Lynn looked uncomfortable, but I stared at her until she spoke. "Well, no, I think the exact words used, in general, by most people, were, 'Sherlock Holmes nutter,' but that's not to say some people, one person actually, didn't use the word 'disciple,' right?"

Whatever. Following Sherlock Holmes principles made me beyond amazing at my job, which allowed me to live on my own, without having to share my personal space with intruders such as flatmates. It wasn't luxury, but there was a door between the sleeping space and the living space, and it was in a good location.

I didn't say anything. I knew she had something to tell me, but I didn't want to make it easy for her. I assumed her issue was personal, but beyond that I didn't know. She hadn't been the nicest person to me so far, and I didn't see why I should be nice to her.

"So, anyway, I heard you were very much into guessing, I heard you guessed a lot of things right about people you work with, and you have this Sherlock Holmes wallpaper on your laptop, so I thought I might set you to work on this . . . let's call it an inconvenience, I might ask you to work on this inconvenience I have, and see if you can guess what it's about."

I looked at her as disdainfully as I could. "I don't guess," I told her, my tone dripping with ice. "I observe, and I deduce."

Again, she looked taken aback. Come on, she'd worked with me for over a month, hadn't she learned who I was, and how I talked by now, not to mention my strong preference for using the perfect exact words for one's thoughts?

I made my contempt as palpable as possible, but she didn't crumple. Most people got flustered when I set my mind to it, and a part of me was impressed. I scolded myself. If I let her impress me, I'd end up falling for her. Women who weren't impressed by my skills, women who were as smart, or smarter, than I was, and mostly women who stood up to me and didn't take any of my shit were like catnip to me. And yes, this had been discussed in therapy. At length. Moving on.

Instead of crumpling, Lynn slid a small envelope face down across the table, and I looked at her interrogatively.

"I received it Saturday," she said, "and I want you to figure out what it's about."

No please, no asking, just an order.

"Is it personal or professional?"

"I don't know," Lynn said, and for a second, she seemed vulnerable.

"Why would I help you with something that might be personal?"

"Because it's a challenge for you, and from what I hear, you don't back down from a challenge."

"Normally, if I try to deduce something, no one knows about it. I don't broadcast anything I find, at least not on purpose, because I don't want to hurt people on purpose, but I do tend to put my foot in my mouth a lot because I see things in black and white."

Lynn stood and planted her palms on the table in front of her. "Abigail Palmer, let me make something very clear. If you *don't* take on this 'case,' I will get you booted off this project faster than you can say 'enhancement,' and then out of the whole company. You will be out on your ass. And if you tell anyone about this arrangement, the consequences will be the same."

* * *

My brain froze for a second while I processed her threats, then my hand slithered across the table to the envelope. I tentatively took it from the sides, trying to handle it as little as possible, just in case there were fingerprints, or DNA, or anything.

The envelope itself was white, in a heavy stock paper, and tiny, the kind you'd get with a florist-delivered bunch of flowers. It was addressed to L. James, no address.

I looked up to Lynn. "Where did you get this?"

"It was waiting for me yesterday when I got home from work."

"You live locally?"

Lynn nodded yes and I let it sink in. Winburyton was tiny, and I found it odd that I'd never met her in town before. Or maybe I had, but hadn't realised.

I carefully opened the envelope and extracted a heavy-stock card, again like you'd get from a florist, but devoid of any markings or logo. In capital block letters, written in wobbly thick pencil were the words:

Tell the truth or I will

Below the sentence was a symbol, six triangles arranged in a circle, reminding me of a stylised drawing of a sun.

I flipped the card over. "That's it?" I asked Lynn. "What's this about?"

Her cheeks darkened. "I told you, I don't know. It's up to you to figure it out."

I cautiously put the card back in the envelope and slid it back to the middle of the table.

"No offence, but it sounds like it's for the police, not me. I'm not a detective."

"I don't want to involve the police," Lynn replied, "too much hassle, and I don't have time to deal with that at the moment."

"You must have an idea of what they're talking about," I insisted. If I received this type of note, my mind would immediately jump to two or three possible big things, and quite a lot of little ones. Still, this wasn't about me.

Lynn stood. "No, I don't." And with that, she walked out of the room.

I stared at the envelope.

Where was I supposed to start? There wasn't much to go on, and Lynn had been far from helpful. Dear Sherlock wouldn't be that helpful here, since Mr Doyle had written him as a fully formed, very experienced detective. Only in one of the stories did he reference Mr Holmes's first case, and Mr Holmes didn't have a client who refused to tell him anything about the problem, or about what could lead to the guilty party.

I slid the envelope in my notebook. There was work to do, work that actually paid the mortgage. Hopefully some miracle would happen and I would know what to do with the envelope, which would lead to me not losing my job.

2

For the first time in ten years, my current project was in the small town I lived in, meaning I didn't have to do the typical consultant life where I left for work at crazy o'clock on a Monday morning, and didn't get back home until late Thursday night. If I didn't have midday meetings, I could even go home for lunch.

When other consultants (especially the baby ones, for some reason) asked me if I didn't miss the camaraderie, the hanging out at the bar in the evenings, the shared taxi rides in the morning, my answer was a flat out "no." I'd never particularly liked living in hotels, but ever since I'd started this project, I couldn't imagine going back to that life.

However . . . it had only been a month. Maybe the novelty of being home every night would wear off, eventually, although I doubted it.

A couple of hours after meeting with Lynn, long after the large open-plan office had become a ghost town, I walked away from the industrial estate the client's project office was on.

I could go straight home, and take a closer look at the threat (I'd started calling it a threat about five minutes after leaving the meeting room, because that's what it was, at least to me).

Or I could pop round to the shops, grab a selection of vegs, dips, and tortilla chips, and head over to Hannah's for a catch-up slash bitching session. I texted her, and walked in silence, enjoying the crunch of the fallen leaves underfoot, while I waited for her response.

What would Sherlock Holmes do? He would smell the envelope and the note, detect a faint whiff of a rare perfume, which he would remember smelling on a random woman in a shop, and would deduce she was the one who'd sent the note. Then he'd figure out her connection to Lynn, deduce why she'd sent the note, and then tell all parties what had happened. My problem was, no matter how much I fantasised I was like him, I wasn't, because he was a fictional character. I was nowhere near smart enough to be like him, and do what he did. My phone gently buzzed in my hand.

> **Hannah: all done with work bitching session most welcome**

Hannah was the nicest person I knew but she didn't believe in punctuation. It was like nails on a chalkboard to me, but I'd long ago given up on changing her. I'd known her for what felt like ever. We'd first met at the pub, a night a local cover band was gigging, right before I'd started on the consulting firm's graduate programme. Who knew back then they would turn out to be my forever-employer?

That night, Hannah had been blind drunk after having only two shandies—on account of it being her birthday— and the two friends she'd been with had been hiking her bodysuit up into a thong.

We'd met again at the next gig, and the next one, and eventually bonded over our love of that cover band and the fact neither one of us usually drank alcohol. Being the only two sober people in a pub packed with drunks had a way of bringing people together.

After such a strange meeting, a dose of positivity and optimism from the bubbliest, sparkliest person I knew would be most welcome.

I hiked the messenger bag on my shoulder, tightened my scarf to guard against the mid-October chill, and strode towards town, a podcast running in my ears, eyes on the pavement to avoid tripping on treacherous asphalt-covered tree roots.

* * *

I'd added a bottle of fancy lemonade for Hannah to my shopping list and the hefty bags had dug deep into my hands by the time I reached Hannah's house on a quiet street lined by late nineteenth-century terraced red-brick houses. I ignored the doorbell, knocked, and pushed the door open.

Hannah walked out of the kitchen to greet me and exclaimed, "Oh my, did you buy the whole shop?"

I gave her a big hug. "Just a few nibbles. Judging by your enthusiastic reply, you've had a shit day at the salon?"

She shook her beautiful auburn bob. "You have no idea. This woman came in, and she asked for the same hairstyle as her dog."

I paused, bags lifted in mid-air above the kitchen table, not sure I'd heard her right.

"I swear," Hannah continued. "She had this small white-haired dog with tight curls, and she wanted a rinse to whiten her hair, and then she wanted it set in tight curls just like his. I tried to get her to change her mind, and she called the manager to complain about me." Hannah got two glasses out of the cupboard and set them on the table a bit harder than she would have needed to.

"I was just looking out for her. I did what she wanted in the end, but she looked ridiculous carrying that dog in her arms."

She paused to reflect. "I suppose when the dog is on the ground it's not as bad."

"Did you take a picture?"

Hannah gave me a stern look that said, 'I'm way too nice to sneak a picture of someone who looks ridiculous,' then her face softened. "I didn't, but I kind of wish I did."

We spread out the vegs and dips on the table, and Hannah fetched a bowl for the tortilla chips. "How was your day doing all the high-powered stuff at the biscuit company?"

I smiled. I'd tried to explain to Hannah what I did, but she was still under the impression it was high-powered, because of the travelling and the long hours. The reality was on the boring side, my consultancy firm sent me to various companies (the clients), sometimes for long-term assignment, sometimes for very short assignments.

There, I looked at their business processes (how they did things) in the sales and customer services departments, sometimes in the logistics department too, and I helped them improve them, or simplify them, so that when they put their new (and very expensive) enterprise resource planning software system (the computer stuff the people working there used) in place, we (the consultants) could use the standard functionalities, instead of having to create something bespoke (even more expensive), and afterwards, the client's people would have less admin work to do. Win-win.

A side of it suited me, because it was black and white, and it required some mental gymnastics to understand a client's processes and come up with better ways that also fit with the future computer systems, but I hated the other side of it, which was that I had to talk to a lot of people, and spend a lot of time with them. I didn't like people.

"The biscuit company is fine," I said. "By the way, I have access to the staff shop, so let me know if you want anything at seventy-five percent discount." I saw a glimmer shine in Hannah's eyes.

"Oh, yes please. Just take whatever you think I'll like."

I mentally rolled my eyes. Hannah, for some odd reason, always assumed that whatever I did or picked was the best. "Is there anything you don't like? Flavour? Texture?"

"I don't like the mousse-y textures. And I'm not too keen on pistachio. Apart from that, anything goes."

"Dark chocolate? Milk? White?"

She crinkled her nose in disgust. "Definitely not dark."

I made a mental note as I dipped a carrot stick in beetroot hummus. "As for your other question, something weird happened today." I told her what had happened with Lynn, and she clapped with glee.

"That's perfect for you, you can be a detective, like Veronica Mars, or Nancy Drew, or your all-time hero, Sherlock Holmes!"

"I'm not sure about that to be honest . . .. There's really not much to go on, and Lynn won't tell me what it's about."

I put a handful of tortilla chips on my plate and dipped one in the cheese sauce. It tasted heavily processed, but something about it was comforting. Maybe the high fat content. Maybe the preservatives.

"Can you show me?" Hannah asked.

I went to wash my hands at the sink (didn't want greasy fingerprints on what could be a key piece of evidence in a future trial) and pulled out the note.

Hannah stared at it for a minute. "That's it?"

"That's it. Like I said, not much to go on."

"What's that symbol?" She pointed at the stylised sun drawing at the bottom.

"No idea. I've been thinking about it all afternoon, and it looks familiar, but I can't put my finger on it."

"You've seen it before?"

I nodded. "I think so, but where or when, that is the question. Maybe I just need to sleep on it and the answer will come to me in the morning." I took a sip of lemonade and winced. Way too sweet for me. "I might try to canvass the local florists Saturday morning, see if they carry those cards and envelopes. It's a long shot, but I've got to start somewhere."

"Do you want me to pop down tomorrow?" Hannah asked. "I'm not working in the morning, and you'll have the answer faster."

I considered her offer while munching on a cauliflower floret. It would make my life easier, but if something happened to the envelope, for whatever reason, I didn't want it to hurt our friendship. And I knew myself, I would hold her responsible if something did happen. Hannah was a lot more relaxed about things than I was, and that was one of the reasons I loved her so much, but at the same time, I often thought she was *too* relaxed and casual about things.

"Don't worry about it," I said, "Lynn didn't seem particularly worried about the note, more annoyed I'd say. It can wait till Saturday."

I put the note back in my bag, and out of my mind. Mostly. "Oh, I forgot."

Hannah's cheese sauce-covered tortilla chip froze mid-air. "What?"

I grinned. "I also bought cake."

3

When I closed the door to my flat behind me, I leaned against it and exhaled. I was home. My sanctuary. A safe haven where no one but me—and occasionally Hannah—ever entered. This was my space.

Jasper came to greet me, tail in the air, meowing that I had abandoned him. He was usually quite chilled, tonight's outrage was unusual.

"Hello kitty cat," I said while I emptied my messenger bag. "Sorry I'm late, but I fear you're going to have to get used to it."

I hung my coat and scarf, kicked off my shoes before stroking Jasper's head on the way. Water bottle and lunch box went to the kitchen—I sometimes dreamed they'd walk there on their own— and I returned to the living room. I laid note and envelope side by side on the table and stared at them for a minute. If only I could remember where I'd seen that symbol before.

I went to give the water bottle a good rinse and left it to drain before donning an apron and tackling the dishes. This was routine, in the purest sense of the word. I repeated those actions every night without fail, in the same order. Routine gave me comfort, but it also meant everything that had to be done got done. Tonight, it had the added bonus of freeing up my mind.

I ran the water until it was hot enough and added a

squirt of dishwashing liquid to the sponge, letting my mind roam. I needed to remind Paul his last three integration functional specs were due at the end of the week. I also needed to buy milk, eggs, and bread. Really should have done that tonight while I was at the supermarket. Maybe I could pop out at lunchtime tomorrow, wander round the shops in town.

That was one thing that I really liked about Winburyton, it had all the usual suspects in term of high-street retailers, but it was also chock-full of independent retailers, who, for the most part, had been there for decades, and were striving.

For the bread, I'd go to Alice's bakery. I wondered if she still did the walnut-studded wholemeal bread. And the autumn-special pumpkin-and-sage buns, actually shaped like pumpkins, adorable and delicious. For the eggs and milk, I'd go to Black's, and get some cheese at the same time. Maybe get some fruits and vegs from Sam's, although my weekly veg box was due Friday. Maybe just fruits. Maybe some plums, then I could make an autumn crumble. I had a few apples left, that would do nicely. I needed to remember to get more cinnamon and nutmeg. I shook the water off the last dish and set it on the draining board.

There was something satisfying about doing the dishes: you started with a full and messy sink, and you ended up with a full and tidy draining board full of gleaming dishes. A small comfort in life.

I added some biscuits to Jasper's bowl, and went to check for the second time that I had locked the front door properly before reviewing tomorrow's calendar. Great. Another day where I wouldn't have time for lunch. I walked back to the kitchen, dropping my laptop on the table on the way, and got a clean lunchbox out. Okonomiyaki, my favourite Japanese omelette, and some onigiri, those moreish Japanese rice balls filled with anything you wanted, would do nicely. I beat the eggs in a bowl relishing the mindless motion. Mindless up to a certain point.

"Shit"

I'd been a tad too enthusiastic and had sloshed half of the eggs on the counter. Some had splashed on the apron. That's what it was for. I got a new egg out of the fridge and started beating again.

The symbol looked so familiar, it had to be a logo of some kind, and I would have had to have seen it before, more than once or I wouldn't have remembered it, but not *that* often, or I would have known what it was straightaway.

I poured some of the egg mixture in the hot pan. Maybe I should make a list. If I'd seen the symbol in town, maybe listing all the shops I could think of could help? I rippled the egg on a side of the pan and poured some more. Then I could have a look online to figure out what their logo was, crossing them off the list until I found the right one. More rippling and more egg. That was assuming it was a local shop logo. What if I remembered it because I'd seen an ad somewhere?

I turned the gas off under the pan and rolled the okonomiyaki before slicing it and carefully setting each roll in the lunchbox. I put some sushi rice to cook and sat at the table. The list was going to be long if I were to list every shop in town, but I could probably ignore those I went to frequently. Maybe I shouldn't focus on just the town centre though. There were some shops on the commercial estate bordering the town, and while I rarely went there, maybe I'd seen a delivery van driving around.

Instead of listing every shop from memory, I looked up a list online. By the time I was done crossing out the shops I knew were not the one I was looking for, the rice was done. I drained it and pushed little balls in the shaper, not before sliding some pickled ginger in the middle first. Job done, I hung the apron back on its hook and returned to the table, letting the balls cool in their mould.

Jasper jumped on my lap with an imperative meow.

"Oh no, Jasper, not while I still have my work clothes on." Jasper purred loudly in reply, blissfully shedding multi-coloured hair all over my black trousers and white shirt. I should have thought it through before getting a tortoiseshell kitten. The no-longer kitten-like Jasper head-butted me in the chin, demanding attention. I absent-mindedly scratched his head while going through shops' websites on my laptop and crossing out those that didn't remotely match.

Jasper's tail flickered, then swished harder and harder. "What? You're on my lap and I'm petting you, why aren't you happy? Is it because you don't have my undivided attention?"

In response, Jasper turned around on my lap, pushing his butt in my face, then turned around again, tail furiously swishing.

"No—" I didn't have time to stop it. In one fell swoop, Jasper's tail had brushed over the table and pushed all the papers on the floor, threatening note and envelope included. I dove to the ground, ejecting a furious Jasper in the process. I wasn't a bad housekeeper per se, I definitely didn't live in squalor, but when work got busy, vacuuming and mopping the floors did take quite a bit of a back seat, and there was always the possibility that

Jasper had done one of his specialities: the invisible throw-up that you *could* detect by smell, but could only find by accidentally stepping in it.

Everything looked fine, but, as I lightly brushed the threat note with the side of my hand, I felt a slight indentation across the card. I held it sideways to the light, and there was no doubt, there was writing embossed on the card.

I pulled a blank sheet of paper from the printer tray and said a silent thank you to past me for having bought the cheapest paper available, thin and a little bit see-through, perfect for what I wanted to do. I laid the card on the table and covered it with the paper, then took my hardest pencil, a relic from the time I thought I could learn to draw. Very gently, holding the pencil almost parallel to the paper I rubbed the graphite tip across the page, holding my breath the whole way, waiting to see if anything would happen. Nothing did, except that the area on the paper was now shaded grey all over. I repeated the task, pushing a bit harder on the pencil. Writing appeared diagonally across the card. Chances were the threatener hadn't realised he'd left a mark on the card. I re-shaded the area until the markings were crystal clear.

29687

Five digits. If I were a cartoon character, a bunch of question marks would be popping over my head like soap bubbles on a summer day. Another lead. But what did it mean? With this note, it felt like every lead led straight into a wall.

I got up from the table and petted Jasper. "Good cat.

Maybe I should have named you Dr Watson, for your assistance with this case was invaluable," I said in what I imagined Holmes' tone would be.

In the kitchen, I finished preparing my lunch, pushing each rice ball out of its mould and wrapping it in a nori leaf before putting it in the lunch box. I had proteins, carbs, I needed to add some greens. I raided the bag I'd brought back from Hannah's. I weighed each portion of vegetables, making sure each counted as one of my five a day before cramming them in the lunch box. I poured some soy sauce in the tiny fish shaped bottle I'd gotten on my last trip to the Japanese shop in London, then put the lot, bento box, sauce, chopsticks and a dishtowel into my plastic bag dedicated to lunches, before returning the package to the fridge. Ready to go in the messenger bag before I left in the morning.

Back in the living room, I stared at the five digits. The card had to have been underneath another piece of paper, but what? Should the five digits be read individually, grouped together, or in chunks? The combinations were mind-boggling. Maybe I should ask Lynn in the morning. I should also find out more about her and her life. If she wanted my help, she was going to have to do something to help herself too, dammit.

4

I'd left earlier than usual that Tuesday morning, hoping to corner Lynn before she dove into her 7.30am meeting. It felt strange, to be walking mostly alone in relative darkness, constantly readjusting my woollen scarf against the morning chill, only passing the odd dog walker or car. I liked how quiet the world was at this hour, but a part of me felt uneasy, vulnerable.

When the biscuit manufacturing plant's roofs came in sight, I quickened the pace. Almost there, and I wouldn't be a potential prey anymore.

I waved at the security guard as I swiped my pass and went straight up to the project office. No time for a detour via the client's fancy coffee machine (reserved for VIPs, as we—the consultants—had been repeatedly told).

As expected, at 7:15 a.m., the cavernous warehouse-turned-office was almost entirely devoid of people. Lynn wasn't there yet, so I dumped my bag on my favourite desk and booted up the laptop before taking my lunch to the minuscule adjoining kitchen. No fancy coffee meant a slightly funny-tasting cup of Earl Grey instead. I wish they'd fix the water pipes, but this was only a temporary kitchen, set up for the duration of the project, so one could dream.

Walking back past the rows of empty desks with my tea and a small stack of biscuits, I was, even after all these years of doing project after project, filled with a sense of wonder. So many people, banded together for months and years to deliver an IT project.

Often, on new projects, you met people from a previous one, and if they'd been good in the past, and you'd gotten on well, it was a pleasure. After multiple projects, you could even have developed a shorthand that made everything faster, smoother. On the other hand, if they were rubbish, or you disliked each other intensely, then you knew to expect hell for the whole project and prayed the resourcing gods would reassign you fast.

As I walked by her desk, I nodded at Millie, one of the change management people, responsible for making sure the client's employees thought it was a great idea to put in a brand-new computer system that they had no idea how to use in place of their trusted old one that they loved to hate.

She leapt from her chair and in two bounds she was at my side. "Hey Abs, good morning, how are you?"

I flinched. The change people were creatures I disliked in general. Way too touchy-feely. Way too much enthusiasm. Way too much, full stop. "Hi Millie, my name is Abigail, remember? I'm good thank you, how are you?"

Millie's hands flew to her mouth in mock horror. "Oh, I'm so sorry, I keep on forgetting, Abigail." She detached each syllable in a way that made me want to punch her. Why didn't people get that my name was Abigail and that I didn't want to be called Abs, Abby, Gail, or the one that followed me through all secondary school, Biggie. Yes, maybe I had been a bit more than chubby as a teenager, but hormones, an unhappy life, loneliness, and a small allowance that allowed me to buy all the chocolate biscuits in Poundland had been a straight path to a size eighteen.

Millie seemed to be escorting me to my desk, babbling about us having to review the high-level training plan or something. I nodded along until we reached my desk and interrupted her after carefully setting down the mug of steaming fragrant tea and the plate of biscuits.

"Why don't you set up a meeting Millie? Then you can have my undivided attention for an hour," I said with a smile I hoped looked sincere.

She looked taken aback, as if making an appointment hadn't occurred to her. "Sure. When's good for you?"

"My calendar's up to date, just take a look and book when's convenient." Millie's shoulders drooped and reminded me of the look my cat, Jasper, gave me when he realised I was going back out in the evening instead of curling up on the sofa. "You know how to check people's calendar's right?"

"Err, yeah, of course," Millie said brightly. "Let's have a look at yours now." She edged past me, her arm brushing against my breast and made a beeline for the mouse.

I put my hand on hers to stop her. "What are you doing?"

"Checking your calendar."

I discretely exhaled to mask the groan rising up in my throat. "Let's get back to your desk, I'll show you." I abandoned tea and biscuits, and marched her to her laptop.

"So, create a new meeting invite," I instructed, "add me, 'Finance' Peter too, and from the business we'll need . . . err."

I took a minute to think. I hated useless meetings, and always did my best to consider whether a person would bring anything to a meeting, or would benefit from listening in. If the answer was no to both, then they were not invited.

Also, why had I never before wondered why we, the consultants, lumped all of the client's employees under one generic term, 'the business', while the client's employees who worked on the project used 'the business' to refer to their colleagues who were not on the project? And why was Millie staring at me?

Oh, right, the invitees. "Get Samira from the business."

I watched her add the names, correcting her when she picked the wrong 'Peter' three times in a row. "Now click there, scheduling," I said.

Her eyes widen as she realised she could now see all the invitees' availability. "That's so convenient, I wish I'd known it was there, it would have saved me so much time. Thank you sooo much Abs! Abigail."

I nodded. Great. I'd seen that face and heard those thanks before. I was now her go-to person for any random question she had. Fantastic. Maybe I could get shipped off to another project. The trade-off between this vapid girl following me around, and not being home every night was a toss-up. She was cute and all, but really not my type. My type was smart. I caught a movement out of the corner of my eye, and spotted Lynn striding towards her desk.

"You're welcome, I've got to catch Lynn, excuse me." No time to smooth out my exit, I had a job to do. Well, another job.

* * *

"Lynn, do you have ten minutes? It's about the task you assigned me yesterday."

Lynn narrowed her eyes. If she asked who I was I wouldn't be surprised. "Do you mean the latest updates to the process design documents? Is there a problem?"

I forgot I was supposed to review those. Bugger. Never mind, it wouldn't take more than a couple of hours anyway. Boring, yes, but not difficult. I lowered my voice.

"No, I meant the note you received."

Lynn frowned. If I had to take a guess as to what was going on in her mind, it would be something along the lines of, 'why is she bothering me with this, if it's not about work, I don't want to hear about it.'

"Fine, but let's make it quick, I have a call with the guys in India in ten minutes and I still need to prep for the Sunrise meeting."

The Sunrise meeting was when everybody from the project who was based in the UK—as opposed to India, though the team over there had their own Sunrise meeting—all eighty-seven of us, squeezed on one side of the office and stared at billboard-sized charts and graphs pinned to the wall. It was also when all the consultants and about half of the client's people on the project had to condense an update including the good (on track), the bad (blockers they needed help with), and the ugly (it had all gone pear-shaped and they couldn't see a way out) in less than two minutes, so everyone had a chance to speak, and the meeting had to end by 8:59 a.m. latest. One minute over, and everyone's diaries would be in shambles for the rest of the day.

I followed Lynn to a meeting room right off the kitchen and passed the list of digits over to her. "Does this look familiar?"

Lynn barely glanced at the numbers before throwing the paper on the table. "No, what is it?"

"Take a better look, it could be important."

Lynn folded her arms across her chest and leaned back in her chair. I'd done it. Now she *really* was annoyed with me. "Why?"

I didn't understand her. "Correct me if I'm wrong Lynn, but it sounds like you don't care who sent you this note. Or what it means. Either that, or you already know the answer to both questions, and then I don't know why you *blackmailed* me into getting involved." I wouldn't be taken for a fool, and I was done playing employee of the month. By involving me, she'd made me a detective, and as a detective, I had to investigate. Plus, I'd never met a question I didn't want an answer to, a mystery I didn't want to work out, a problem I didn't want to solve.

Lynn's cheeks darkened to a deep burgundy. "How dare you talk to me like this? I'm going to have you booted off this project."

A wave of calm engulfed me. "No you won't," I said very quietly. "You would need to explain why, and you know I'd tell them about the note." Lynn's face fell. I had been right. I had called her bluff. "Take a seat. Answer my questions."

Lynn obeyed, defeated. I could tell from her body language she really wasn't happy about no longer being in the driver's seat. Lynn was a control freak, which was what made her a very good project manager, and a horrible boss.

"Now, look at those numbers again: 29687. You worked on the Continent and in the US. These could be a post code. Does it ring a bell?"

"I don't know. Really." Arms crossed in front of her, shoulders rounded, she stared at the numbers.

I tried to be nicer. "Lynn, you must have thought there was something real about this note, or you wouldn't have asked for my help." Or blackmailed me into looking into it.

"I don't know. I thought I saw someone lurking in front of the house a few times in the past couple of weeks, and I guess that's why I thought the note was a bigger deal than it was."

Alarm bells rang in my head. "Lynn, if you have a stalker, you have to go to the police. No ifs or buts, you have to go."

She tightened her jaw. "And what if it's nothing? They'll laugh at me."

I changed tacks. "Let's look at it from a different angle." I put the envelope, address side up, on top of the numbers. "Who lives at your address?"

Lynn looked confused. "I don't see how that's relevant—"

"Lynn. You have three options. Either you go to the police, or you do nothing and ignore the note, or you answer my questions and let me help you dammit."

Her mouth rounded in a perfectly shocked 'O'.

At work, I did my best to avoid swearing, and to keep my temper in check, but I had a short fuse, and Lynn's lack of cooperation had reached the limits of my patience. "I can drop it and get back to my life if you've changed your mind, that's fine by me."

Silence floated in the room, only broken by the loud tick-tock of the analog wall clock. I counted sixty-nine ticks before Lynn spoke again.

"There's me, obviously, my husband Elliott, and my grandfather-in-law lives in the annex."

I forgot to breath for a couple of seconds. I knew that as project manager she made more than, me, but I hadn't realised quite how much more. "You have an annex? Where do you live, a mansion?"

She leaned away from the table. "It's just a regular house, but we converted the double-car garage into a small apartment when my father-in-law passed a few years ago. Lester was living with him, so he moved in with us."

"Lester?" I couldn't believe my ears.

"Yes, my grand-father-in-law. My husband's grandfather."

I took a deep breath, trying to steel myself to not yell at her about how useless she was. "Lynn. The envelope. It's addressed to L. James. Not Lynn James, *L.* James."

She looked at me expectantly, waiting for me to spell it out for her. If I'd rolled my eyes, I would have seen the back of my head. "Couldn't the L stand for Lester?"

I watched the penny drop and Lynn burst out laughing, a big laugh that could have been infectious if it hadn't sounded a bit insane and hysterical. Watching her felt sad, not joyous.

I put the envelop and the note back in my notebook before walking out of the room. I turned on the cold water tap in the minute kitchen, nodding hello to the steady stream of people passing through on their way to the project office, and poured Lynn a glass of water. When I walked back into the room, she was dabbing her eyes with a crumpled tissue.

She took a sip. "Thanks."

I checked the clock. "You've got a call to go to, but this conversation isn't over."

5

The rest of the morning had been okay. Productive at least. Lynn had done her utmost possible to avoid me, which was fantastic. The less she was on my back, the more I got done. I'd mostly successfully hidden from Millie, who, as predicted, had tried to latch on after deciding that I was the mentor she needed or something. I was nobody's mentor. I worked alone. I tolerated competent people around me, but that was it.

And now, finally, it was time for a very late lunch break. Or break, without lunch. I wanted to do some shopping in town. And ideally go home after, but that was wishful thinking. I shrugged into my coat and checked the time. Later than I thought. I'd have to walk quickly if I wanted to get everything I needed before the shops closed. I hurried out the office and was at the top of the stairs when Peter, the senior finance consultant, stopped me.

"Abigail."

So close, and yet so far. I could kiss my crusty sourdough and my goat's cheese Gouda goodbye. I plastered a smile on my face. "Peter, how lovely to see you. I was just on my way out; can it wait until I'm back?"

Peter made an impression of a goldfish breaking the water surface to kiss the air while the question wormed its way through his brain. "It's about this meeting Millie set up, the one she sent an invite for this morning. If we're talking training, I need to invite Jackie too. She's one of our key stakeholders in the business, so we want to make sure she's as involved as possible."

I wondered why Peter had come to me instead of Millie, since she was the one who'd set up the meeting. I didn't like his tone, I always felt like, to him, I was a secretary in the seventies. Nineteen-seventies.

I shook my head and tried to keep the contempt out of my voice. "This is just an exploratory meeting. We're going to throw a bunch of ideas to the ceiling and see what sticks. Chances are everything will flop. You really don't want Jackie in there for that, right?"

"You got Samira in there representing the Sales team in the business, so why not Jackie?"

I'd tried my best to be polite, but I had no idea why he was sounding so aggressive. "I get it Peter, but Samira is really good at generating ideas, and at working with us to improve on our ideas. For Jackie, I think it's better if we go to her later, maybe next week, with a few ideas, let's say five, for which we have implementation plans. Jackie doesn't like the messy design process, she likes to have clean products."

Peter retreated a couple of steps, back towards the office. "Fine, if you say so."

"See you later," I called out as I slowly walked down the stairs. No point in hurrying up, it was now 2:35 p.m., the bakery closed at three, and I was twenty-eight minutes' walk from town. Goodbye cosy bread-and-cheese evening.

Why did people always do that, I wondered, catch you right when you're leaving the office, and you're in a hurry? Maybe it wouldn't matter if I didn't have the fresh fluffy bread. The cheese on its own would be nice too. It wasn't like I'd *needed* the bread. I pushed the side door out to the car park, absent-mindedly keeping it open for an invisible person, out of habit, and Millie squeezed right behind me.

"Bye Abigail, have a lovely evening."

Did that girl's energy and enthusiasm know no limits?

"It's barely mid-afternoon, I'm coming back," I replied in what I thought was a pleasant enough tone, but Millie stopped mid-bound.

"What's wrong? You sound all disappointed and flat."

"Well, yes, I am. I had made some very unexciting plans for tonight, but Peter held me up and I've missed my window." I shrugged. "I'll survive, it's not the end of the world."

"Oh nooo." Millie made a pretend sad face. "What were you going to do?"

I shook my head. I didn't want to tell her, she'd think it was boring and unexciting, and then she'd tell everyone on the project how boring and unexciting I was.

"Go on, if it was important to you, then it has to be interesting."

Maybe I'd dismissed Millie's abilities too soon. The girl knew how to extricate information out of people. I gave her a half-smile. "I was going to go to the bakery and the cheesemonger in town to get some really nice foods and have a comfy evening at home, but, since I walked in this morning instead of taking the car, I won't make it before the shops close."

"Oh, is that it?" Millie exclaimed. No, my original assessment of the girl had been right. Airhead. "That's no big deal, I'll drop you off, just tell me the way."

I cocked my head to the side, not sure I'd heard her right. "Excuse me?"

Millie beeped a little baby-blue car open. "I'll drop you off," she repeated, "get in, quick, then you'll even have time to taste some new cheeses you've never tried before."

She paused, eyes slightly glazed over before coming back in focus. "I love cheese. Except the bland ones. What's the point of bland cheese? And diet cheese. Same thing. What's the point? If it doesn't have fat in it, it's not cheese," she said vigorously. She opened the boot, threw her bag in unceremoniously and hopped in the car while I stood rooted to the spot.

The girl liked cheese. The girl had *opinions* about cheese. Maybe I would let her ask me questions after all.

I climbed in the passenger seat.

"Right, you'll need to tell me where I'm going," Millie said as we waited for the car park barrier to raise, "I only know the bit between the dual carriageway and the car park entrance."

"Just turn left instead of right here," I said. "How long have you been on this project?"

"Since the beginning," she said brightly, "so coming on three months now."

"I can't believe you've never explored the town," I said, barely trying to mask my disapproval.

"Never had the time or the opportunity really. You know how it is, work, go for dinner with colleagues, go to the hotel bar with colleagues, go to bed, repeat."

"Sure, but you could try going for dinner in town, there are some cool restaurants there. Heck, there's a pizzeria that's run by an Italian guy who makes cheese-stuffed crust pizzas that will make you cry they're so good."

Millie eyed me from the side while taking on a round-about a bit faster than I would have liked. "No pizza can be that good."

"Giuseppe's Pizza is the best pizza restaurant I've ever been too, and you can bet that after ten years of being a consultant, I've been to a few."

"Maybe we could all go on Thursday, blow off some steam at the end of the week, maybe go for drinks afterwards? I'm sure we can get taxis arranged."

I hated team dinners, unless they were with a very select few people who didn't make me feel like I had to play a role for the duration of the outing. "The place is quite small, we definitely wouldn't all be able to fit there."

Millie didn't respond. Her face was as neutral as I'd ever seen it. Maybe she was focused on the driving? Or maybe she'd interpreted my words as a criticism? That seemed to happen a lot with me. Maybe I should try to encourage her a little. "It was a good idea though."

"Doesn't matter. The dragon lady probably wouldn't have approved the taxis anyway."

"Turn left here. Dragon lady? Do you mean Lynn?"

"Yeah. I can't stand that woman. I don't think anyone can, really. It looks like she's talking to you like a normal person, and the next minute you get burned from the fire she breathed on you."

"Lynn? She's a control freak, but I'd never have thought to compare her to a dragon. You can just drop me off anywhere around here," I said.

"Over the summer she publicly humiliated me for wearing flip-flops. In front of the whole office. Including the client people."

No idea why, but I pictured Millie turning up to the office in thick-foam-soled flip-flops topped with pink, sequined flowers. "Okay, maybe she could have been a bit more tactful, but flip-flops aren't exactly office attire, are they?"

"They were brown leather," Millie exclaimed, indignant. "Perfectly office-appropriate. No one had noticed them until she made a big show of pointing them out."

"I'm sorry," I said. And I was. Public humiliation for the sake of it was the kind of thing a deeply insecure or fundamentally mean person would do. I had made people cry before, but never on purpose, never out of malice. It hadn't happened that often, but when it had, it was when I was giving carefully crafted constructive criticism, and the person had taken it like a personal attack on them. If people couldn't separate personal attacks and professional development opportunities, there wasn't much I could do about it.

Millie stopped the car at a bus stop and I turned to her. "I'm sure she didn't want to hurt your feelings. She probably views even the smallest toe cleavage as unprofessional. I'm not defending her, she should definitely have spoken to you privately about it, she didn't handle it well."

"Maybe, but that's only one example. Everybody who's ever worked with her has at least one. She's pure evil."

* * *

The dashboard clock indicated it was already 2:52 p.m. "Thank you very much for dropping me off Millie, I really appreciate it." I stepped out, and Millie shouted, "Let's do it again soon!" as I slammed the door.

I rushed over to the bakery, run by the same family, the Bramptons, for five generations.

"Hi Abigail," Alice greeted me. "Not working today?"

I liked Alice. We'd been to school together, so I'd known her practically my whole life. We were never friends, but never enemies either. Just people who were aware of each other's existence and peacefully coexisted.

"Haha, I wish. No, I escaped from the office, a colleague was kind enough to give me a lift so I could get here before you closed."

"Well, you made it, so what can I get you?"

I almost always got the same order, but Alice knew better than to assume anything with me. "A crispy baguette, a thick-crust sourdough, a half dozen cinnamon-and-raisin bagels and . . . let's see." I looked through the shelves, trying to see if Alice's dad, the main baker, had come up with anything original.

Alice knew the drill, having been through it enough times. "We've got olive-and-onion fougasses, chilli-cheese-crusted rye breads, wine-and-chorizo breads, cheddar-and-bacon Irish soda breads, and conchas, which are Mexican sweet rolls. Oh, and because it's the season, pumpkin-and-sage buns."

"Wow, you guys really went all out today! I'll have four pumpkin-and-sage buns please. They're so cute!"

Alice collected the breads and rang up the order. "You better hurry if you want to get to Black's before Frank closes."

My lips parted in surprise. "How did you know?"

"Because you never buy this much bread if you don't plan to have a bread-and-cheese feast in front of a soapy movie."

"I'll have you know Legally Blonde is a feminist movie that makes people think," I replied dryly. And I meant it, too. It genuinely was one of my favourite movies, and one I indeed intended to watch that night to remind myself that anything could be achieved if you put your mind to it. I'd been selected as some sort of private detective, it was time I started believing it myself, and Reese Witherspoon was going to help me achieve that.

I waved goodbye to Alice and speed-walked to Blacks across the street, silently praying Frank didn't have a date tonight and wouldn't have closed early.

He spotted me through the plate glass window as he handed a customer their bag of goodies, and his eyes widened. It didn't take a mind-reader to know what he was thinking. *Not her, please, no, she'll be here forever.*

I always felt like I was a nightmarish customer for him, because I always wanted to try all the weird and wonderful cheeses he had, and I always took a tiny little bit longer than the average customer who just wanted Brie for six people or a whole Camembert for baking.

"Hi Frank, how are you doing?"

"Same old, same old," he replied morosely. I liked him, because underneath his grumpy outside, there was a real cheese expert, and I'd discovered some wonderful ones thanks to him. "What can I do you for?"

"I need half a pound of the salt crystal butter, and then some cheeses. Oh, and I'll get a small box of eggs please."

Frank nodded and set to cutting the butter. "Which eggs do you want? Organic? Omega-3? Cheapest?"

I did a quick mental review of what I'd eaten that week, decided I really should have eaten more oily fish, and settled on the Omega-3-enriched eggs. I didn't know if they really were that different from the regular eggs, but, supposedly, Omega-3s boosted brain power, and I thought I would need all the extra power I could get.

"And what cheeses?"

"Let's see, I'll start with a goat's milk Gouda and the chilli Cheddar."

"Sorry, I'm all out of that Gouda."

A cloud of disappointment settled over my head. "Oh." I'd been looking forward to it, and now, I was a bit flustered. I took a deep breath. No way was I going to have a meltdown at the cheesemonger's. "What else do you recommend?"

Frank rolled his eyes, knowing I wouldn't take offence, and started pointing at wheels and packaged cheeses in the glass refrigerated case. "I've got this new blue, a Cheddar from a small supplier, and an aged Parmesan."

"I'll have all three."

Frank froze in shock. I'd never been so quick to decide in my whole life, but I had to get back to the office, get all my work done, and hopefully get home at a decent time, where I would curl up on the sofa with Jasper, Legally Blonde, good bread, and good cheese.

"Everything all right?" Frank asked.

"It's been a long day, and it's far from over yet, that's all."

"Aah. Well, I won't complain, I've got a date with a smoking-hot brunette tonight, and I want to get out of here as soon as possible to get to the gym."

I cocked my head in disbelief. Frank's muscles were so well defined, he could have served as an anatomy model. Even with his clothes on.

He lifted his sleeve all the way up to the shoulder and flexed his biceps. "I want to make sure she's impressed."

I'd never been into muscles much, and thankfully very few women had dedicated their lives to have big muscles like that. Frank turned to let me admire the back of his biceps (or was it his triceps?), and my breath caught in my throat. A tattoo was peeking out of his rolled-up shirt sleeve, and what I could see of it matched the symbol on Lynn's note exactly.

"Hey Frank, does Lynn James ever shop here?"

Frank cocked his head to the side, dumbfounded. "Who?"

"Lynn James. She's black, early forties, a bit shorter than me, probably about five feet four, maybe five five, average figure, black hair cropped super short. Big boobs."

"Oh, yeah, no, she's never been in here, why?"

"She's the project manager where I work, and I thought I could bring her a few of her favourite cheeses," I lied. "I need a favour from her."

Frank finished wrapping the cheeses and passed them over the counter. "Sorry love, can't help you there. Maybe she's one of those weirdos who's allergic to dairy. Or maybe she's on a no-fat diet." He added up my order on his old-fashioned till and glanced blankly at me. "Who knows."

"How much do I owe you," I said brightly.

"That will be twenty-one pounds sixty, thank you very much."

I winced a little. Yes, I'd added butter and eggs, but that was still quite a bit more than I usually spent. Hey, I thought, some people spent that much on steak, I had a good job, I was allowed to treat myself once in a blue moon. Or every week, a little voice in my head said.

I hiked the grocery bag on my shoulder and was ready to leave when words came out of my mouth. "Hey Frank, the tattoo on your arm, what does it mean?" *Damn you brain, you were supposed to filter this kind of stuff.*

Frank frowned. "Which one?"

"The left one."

"No, I mean which tattoo? I have loads."

"I just saw a bit of it when you were showing me your muscles, it looked like triangles going in circles."

"Ha! I'm afraid it doesn't mean anything love, except that you should never go to a tattoo studio after an all-day session in the pub with your mates. I'll tell you what, I woke up the next morning wondering why my arm ached so much, then I looked in the mirror, and there it was. All my mates got it too, we looked like right pricks when we were lined up, I'll tell you."

I wished Frank a good date and left. Walking back to the office, I couldn't help wondering if it was Frank's tattoo that had looked familiar, or if it was someone else's. Maybe I should go back tomorrow, and see if he could remember who else had had the tattoo. And maybe get some more cheese.

6

The next day had started pretty well with a cancelled meeting, freeing up some time to do actual work.

I was in a deep flow when the calendar icon on the taskbar flashed orange, reminding me Millie's meeting was starting imminently. Crap. I'd forgotten about it, and could really do without. Still, she'd made the effort of doing it at a time when it didn't clash with any other meeting in my calendar, the least I could do was show up on time. I grabbed my water bottle and notebook and headed off.

I sat down with everybody else, and very quickly, my mind wandered, returning to Lynn, the note, and how I could figure out more about her life. This was one of the few instances when not being on social media hindered me. Most of the time, I was very happy with having closed all my accounts several years ago, but on days like these, it could have come in handy.

"What do you think Abigail?" Millie asked.

Shit. I hadn't listened to a word. "I think it's an interesting idea that's worth more discussion."

"So, you agree with Peter that we should train the users three months before go-live?"

From Millie's tone, I could tell I was busted. Still, she'd given me an escape ladder, and I was going to climb my way out of the hole.

"I don't, actually, I think we should train them as close to go-live as humanly possible, but I would be interested to hear more from Peter about why he thinks that." Fingers crossed he hadn't already explained the whole thing.

Peter straightened in his chair, as if to give himself more gravitas. "Well, near go-live, we have a lot of users on annual leave, and we wouldn't want them to miss out, surely? So it would make sense to train them when they're all available, then we can get them all in one room and be done with it."

I blinked. How long had Peter been a consultant? He was older than me, and even if he hadn't started as a graduate, chances were he'd been doing project work for at least fifteen years, though a more realistic figure was probably twenty years. Why would he be spewing such inanities? And how did I tell him while also being diplomatic?

"I see your point Peter"—Millie made to interrupt, but I put my hand on her arm to stop her—"however, let me ask you a question. How many users do you have in the Finance space? In the Sales function, we have approximately seventy-five, if we include the external sales teams." I glanced at Samira to make sure I hadn't muddled up the numbers and she nodded in agreement.

"We have eighteen. So what?" Peter said.

"Right. Let me ask you. In your many years of consulting, when did you ever see every single user registered for a training *actually* show up? There's always going to be someone off sick or having to cover childcare at the last minute. Plus, eighteen people in a training session is a bit much, ideally we keep them under ten people."

"I don't care, I don't deal with training. That's why we have trainers and change bunnies," he said, gesturing at Millie. My hand was still on her arm, and I could feel her muscles tense so much I thought she was going to explode.

Yes, we called them *change bunnies*, but not to their faces.

Peter carried on. "We all know how she gets the users to adopt the new system anyway, short skirts, low cleavage, lots of makeup, a little touch here, a laugh there and boom . . . system is adopted. Change management is a joke."

I wanted to punch him in the face. Nothing else would do. But I had Millie on my right, and Samira on my left, and I most definitely couldn't lose it in front of Samira. She was after all, "the client," and I couldn't break the second rule of consulting again—don't fight in front of the ~~kids~~ client—not after people had complained about me on this very same topic only two days ago. I'd do what I was supposed to: adjourn, then go somewhere else to fight.

"Let's wrap up this meeting."

Peter's voice rose by an octave. "What? Why? We haven't agreed on the training strategy yet?"

I resisted the urge to roll my eyes and turned to Samira, who was frozen in her seat. "Samira, I'll catch up with you later, thank you for coming, and I apologise, this behaviour from any of our consultants is absolutely unacceptable."

Stiffly, she nodded, took her laptop, and fled the room.

"Peter, please apologise to Millie, right now. And you should be glad Jackie wasn't in this meeting, because your idea of giving users three months to forget their training on a new system would not have flown."

Peter's face had turned purple. "Who the hell do you think you are? You can't talk to me like this!"

"Why not? Did you hear yourself talking about Millie?"

"But she's just a—"

I knew I shouldn't, but I couldn't avoid challenging him. "A what, Peter?"

"I have twenty-two years of consulting behind me and I will not have some little hussy treat me with such disrespect."

"Peter, I think it would be best to close this meeting. Be aware that I will be reporting your words to Lynn, and I expect you will be hearing from HR."

Peter rose so fast he threw his chair back. He strode across the room to the door and would have slammed it behind him if it hadn't been equipped with a slow-close mechanism.

"Well, that's that. Millie, I want to apologise, and remind you that not all consultants are arseholes." As I said the words, I wondered if I was being hypocritical. I didn't think I was an arsehole, but maybe people thought otherwise.

Millie nodded, eyes glistening as if she was on the brink of tears.

"I'm going to go catch Lynn before Peter has a chance to rewrite this meeting. I'll come find you after. Why don't you go get yourself a proper coffee in the cafeteria?" I seemed to always make it worse when I tried to deal with someone crying, so running away was the safer option.

Lynn was busy talking to someone when I got there, so I hovered near her desk until she was done. I'd learned a long time ago that desk-side conversations were almost always short, so it was often worth waiting.

"PDDs?" she asked when she was done.

The last thing on my mind was the process design documents updates. I shook my head no and looked around. Just Jeff, the programme director and Lynn's big boss on the project, at his desk next to hers. No one lurking. "You have a problem, and it could blow up quite bad." In a few words, I reported Peter's words and behaviour.

Lynn leaned back in her chair, and I could tell she was reviewing potential scenarios. Have a stern word with Peter, replace him on the project, report him to his business unit line manager (since Lynn was only his manager on the project), and probably all sorts of combinations I, not being a people manager, couldn't fathom. I really hoped one scenario she didn't consider viable was do nothing.

"I was afraid this might happen again," she said after a few minutes.

"What? Again?"

She nodded. "Keep it to yourself, but the project manager on his previous project gave him a warning after he lost it with a PMO girl."

Jeff interrupted. "That's how he ended up on this project, they reassigned him."

"Oh." As always when eavesdroppers jumped into a conversation uninvited, I was miffed, but since he was my boss's boss, I was unsure how to react. I nodded and asked Lynn, "What are you going to do?"

"I'll have a word with the resourcing guy, see if we can get him reassigned again."

"And?"

"And what?"

"Aren't you going to report him to HR?"

Lynn suddenly looked very tired. "I see where you're coming from, but that wouldn't change anything."

"Excuse me?"

Jeff rolled his chair closer to us and lowered his voice.

"Peter is from the old guard. The world, and society's attitude towards women changed, but he's stuck in the past. If he'd been a smoker in the nineties, when he could have smoked in the office, I can almost guarantee he would still be trying to sneak up a smoke in here."

I slid behind Lynn's chair so I was standing between the two of them. "Do me a favour, go on the intranet." Jeff raised an eyebrow. "I have a point, I promise." Jeff opened R&G's internal homepage, and I directed him to the news section. "Read the first post at the top," I said. "Please." I had to be careful not to be too directive, Jeff was a big deal in the company, and I'd heard through the grapevine that he'd taken this assignment, which was two grades below him, for personal reasons. Point was, he could make my life hell if he chose to, and potentially terminate my career by blacklisting me with every consultancy firm in the country, and possibly around the world.

Jeff started reading out loud. "Today, we launch our campaign to attract women of all ages to our company, as we recognise they are a mostly untapped talent pool—" He looked up, glanced at Lynn and back to me, and I could tell he'd put two and two together.

"What sort of message does it send if you don't report him?" I asked gently.

Jeff leaned back in his chair and covered his face with his hand before dragging them down, reminding me of Munch's Scream. "Argh."

"I know, but it's the right thing to do."

Jeff looked at me. Or, more exactly, it felt like he was studying me, trying to see into my soul. He glanced over at Lynn before returning to me. "What do you think I should do?" An even tone, probably not a trap.

"Boot him off the project today. Report him to his line

manager and to HR. Call the resourcing people to get a new consultant." He looked at me horrified. "Don't forget Samira, the woman from the client's Sales team, was in there as well. She witnessed and *heard* the whole thing."

"He said that in front of the client?" Lynn spluttered.

I nodded. I had a feeling I'd won this battle, but the feeling of power wasn't pleasant, it was as if a wave submerging me, and I felt drowned, not drunk, with power.

Lynn pushed herself out of her chair. "I'll go find him."

7

I couldn't believe I'd had to fight Lynn and Jeff on this. Reporting Peter was such a no-brainer. And to think that the project manager on his previous project hadn't reported him, had only given him a slap on the wrist? Unbelievable. I dropped my notebook on my desk and sat down before remembering Millie. She wasn't back at her desk. Outside, the rain was falling in thick curtains. I didn't really want to cross the car park to get to the cafeteria in this weather, if she wasn't there. I pulled out my work phone and messaged her.

> Me: Are you still in the cafeteria?
>
> Millie: yes heading back in a sec
>
> Me: Don't, I'm on my way there now.

The lack of punctuation burnt my eyes, but it was something I'd been told to not hold against people. To me, it displayed a lack of care, forcing my brain to work that little bit harder to figure out what the other person meant. Punctuation mattered. If someone texted me, "let's eat children," I'd call the police.

I walked out of the office, grabbing a first come, first served umbrella on the way. Those were really good, the huge golf umbrella kind, so much better than my little folding one. The difference being I could fit mine in my messenger bag, whereas I couldn't fit a golf umbrella. Or I could, but there would be a fair chunk sticking out.

I navigated the car park's puddles as carefully as if they'd been land mines, and climbed the three steps up to the cafeteria.

I set up the coffee machine to treat me to a deliciously foamy cappuccino, put a mug underneath the spout, and looked around for Millie while the espresso god did its job. I spotted her in a far corner, half hidden behind a tall palm plant, nursing a mug of something still steamy.

I sprinkled some cinnamon on my cappuccino and walked over to her table.

I wasn't sure what to say to her, now that I was there. I never knew what to say to people, in general. What was a normal thing to say to someone who'd just been verbally abused?

I sat down across from her at the little round table. "How are you?" She looked at me as if saying 'were we not in the same room?', and kept staring until I spoke. "Yeah, okay, you're not fine."

"You were in there, you heard what he said. It's a miracle I didn't burst out crying. I would have looked like a complete idiot."

I patted her hand. "You wouldn't have. We all would have understood."

"I have to go back, I have meetings, but how am I supposed to face him?"

I debated telling her about my conversation with Lynn and decided not to. The whole thing might have been confidential, and I didn't trust Millie to not blab about it. "The same way you behave every day. You take the high road, hold your head high, and do your job."

"But nobody cares about my job," Millie said in a small voice, and I worried she was going to cry.

I planted my hands on the table and towered over her as I rose from my chair. "Millie, you are absolutely right. People like me, functional consultants, don't care about your job." She opened her mouth in shock, but I didn't give her a chance to interrupt. "Just like you don't give a rat's ass about our jobs. You don't care when we have functional specs due, or if the client has changed their requirements again, or if data is falling apart faster than an ice-cream cake in summer." Millie opened her mouth to contradict me, but quickly shut it. "See, I'm right. It's all a question of perspective. So, go back in there, and go be your annoying self by doing the thing you're paid to do."

"You think I'm annoying?" Millie asked in a small but high-pitched voice. I grabbed my mug of cappuccino and prudently walked away.

8

I brushed my teeth on Thursday morning, and an idea popped into my head. I was going to enlist Hannah and her social media access to figure out what it was Lynn was hiding. Everyone had secrets, or so I'd heard. I had what I liked to think of as flexible secrets. Things that people in my personal life knew, but that I was fiercely keeping under wraps at work. I guessed the opposite was true, but the reason I didn't talk much about work to my friends had less to do with the confidentiality agreements I often had to sign, and more with my not wanting to bore them.

Pulling the curtains open had revealed steady rain so I forwent my trainers and slipped on my work shoes. Bag in one hand, keys in the other, I left the flat with a curious feeling of forgetting something.

My little silver car was waiting for me in its usual spot, gleaming from the rain. I didn't drive it that often, only when it rained, or if I expected to get back from wherever I'd gone particularly late. Winburyton was safe.

Nothing ever happened in Winburyton.

Except for Lynn's letter, but chances were it was someone wanting her to tell the truth about her fat-free pie or something.

I waved at the gatehouse guard while I waited for the car park barrier to lift, inhaling deeply the aroma of hot sugar and spices that wafted all the way from the factory to my half-opened car window. Occasionally other consultants asked me how I didn't put on five pounds just by breathing the air around here. I usually smiled and moved on, for there was no answer to that question. Or more exactly, their problem was a lack of self-restraint. If they'd been content with *smelling* the biscuit-laden air, they wouldn't have a problem. Their problem was that they were on four packs a day. Four packs of biscuits that is. My opinion was that I could have the odd pack every now and then, and it counted as a treat that wouldn't affect my ability to fit into my jeans. But my version of now and then was no more than once a month.

I did have the odd biscuit with tea or coffee in the morning, but I didn't count them because I took the stairs to get to and from the project office, and, due to the office being above a warehouse, they were steeper and had more steps than average. I knew that, because I'd looked it up. Storing useless facts in my brain attic was a given. One that Sherlock Holmes would have me whipped for, since, in his opinion, people had way too much useless stuff up there and didn't retain the important things. That was a fair point, but how were you supposed to know what was important? When in doubt, keep everything, that was my philosophy. Supposedly, we only used ten percent of our brain capacity, so storing useless junk in my brain attic wouldn't be a problem. My brain had expanding storage space.

As I set foot on the first step, my brain switched to work mode. A Pavlovian reflex of sorts. I mentally went through what I had on today. Meetings, meetings, and more meetings. Maybe an uninterrupted two hours' slot in the afternoon that would give me time to review the process design document updates. I'd also need to give a call to—shit.

My curious feeling of forgetting something. I hadn't removed the do-not-disturb on the work phone. Slowing down my walk up the stairs I pulled my phone out and checked the notifications.

Voicemail from Lynn at 10:35 p.m.

I took a deep breath. That was one of the things I really hated about her management style. And that was one of the reasons I set a do-not-disturb block on the work phone overnight. She seemed to believe people were ready and willing to do her bidding twenty-four seven, that they didn't have a life outside of the office. Frequently I'd get emails in the middle of the night from her, mostly unimportant things or reminders to do things that were well in hand, or requesting progress updates. Did she seriously expect she would get a progress update in the middle of the night?

I jabbed the voicemail icon and put the phone to my ear. She'd left an actual message, not a hang-up, so that was something.

Abigail, it's Lynn, call me back as soon as you get this, there was another note waiting for me when I got home.

I hung up and immediately dialled her number. Straight to voicemail. It didn't mean anything, I thought, an uneasy feeling twisting my stomach. She could be in a meeting and have turned off her phone. No, a little voice said in my head, she would have put it on silence, not turned it off completely. Okay, little voice, then maybe she didn't have network. There were a fair amount of dead zones in the Winburyton area, and I still hadn't checked where she lived exactly. Or she could be on another call, that would send me straight to voicemail, right? Or maybe she'd forgotten to charge her phone. No way, the little voice rose up again, a control freak like

Lynn would never in a million years let her phone run out of battery. I shook my head to knock out the little voice that was raising my anxiety levels way beyond manageable. There was nothing I could do in the middle of the stairs, I'd have to see what she wanted when she got to the office. If she got to the office, the little voice whispered. I grumbled and sped up, reaching the door to the office slightly out of breath.

I was one of the first ones in, the drive having taken only five minutes against the thirty-five minutes I'd allocated for my walk, but I couldn't help my gaze turning to Lynn's empty desk anyway. She was normally in early, and she wasn't here yet.

I nodded at the rare few people who d gotten in before me on my way in, not smiling, not wanting to engage in conversations about what antics they'd been up to the night before. I booted up my laptop and pushed Lynn out of mind, burying myself in the gazillions of emails that had mysteriously appeared out of nowhere overnight.

9

At 8:29 a.m., I rose from my chair, steaming mug of tea in one hand, notebook in the other, and followed the flow of people heading for the Sunrise wall.

Jeff, the programme director, was standing by the first tracker pinned to the wall. I frowned. He never led the Sunrise meeting. Sure, he attended, occasionally asked questions no one had answers to, but he never led the meeting. Millie jostled her way through the crowd until she was at my side and elbowed me.

"What's going on?" she whispered. "Where's the witch?"

"The witch?"

"Lynn. She always leads the meeting. No way she delegated."

I tapped my pen against my lower lip. I didn't have an answer for her, but she did have a point. No way would Lynn delegate. My uneasy feeling returned. What if something had happened to her?

The Sunrise meeting came and went, and I swung in and out of meetings all morning, occasionally trying Lynn's phone when I had a few minutes, but always with the same result, straight to voicemail.

At lunchtime, I gathered my courage and went to speak to Jeff. If he'd stepped in to lead Sunrise, he must have known Lynn wouldn't be there, I reasoned, and he would know why.

"Jeff, do you know where Lynn is?" I asked. "She's not picking up her phone."

"Good morning Abigail, I am well, thank you, and how are you?"

I chided myself. Why Jeff always insisted on doing the boring chitchat before getting to the crux of the matter was beyond me. It was a pure waste of time, and people usually regarded it as an open invitation to tell you all about the gastrointestinal issues they'd had the night before. Bleurgh. No thanks.

"Sorry Jeff, a bit stressed out. Good morning, how are you?"

Satisfied that I'd conformed to his ritual, Jeff nodded. "To answer your question, I have no idea where Lynn is. When she didn't show up to update me before Sunrise, I figured she was running late. Now I don't know." His tone sounded reasonably unconcerned, but something about his body language, maybe a slight knitting of his bushy eyebrows made me feel like he was more worried than he let on.

"Thanks. Do let me know if you hear from her, please?"

Jeff raised an eyebrow, as if to say he wasn't my personal assistant, but nodded before turning back to his laptop.

I returned to my desk at a loss. What was I supposed to do? I couldn't call the police, what if it was just that Lynn was sick and had turned off her phone to sleep? I'd look like an idiot, and a time waster. Maybe I should go by her house tonight. I needed to find her address. HR would never give it to me, but maybe she was listed in the white pages. She was old enough that she might still have a landline. And if she didn't, her grandfather-in-law Lester would almost definitely have one.

10

The day dragged on and the too-many meetings drained my social skills' battery. At five, after the last meeting of the day, I pinged Hannah to warn her I'd be coming over later and buried myself in work. Twenty-five minutes later, she pinged back.

> **Hannah: sorry been manic all day I should be home in 30**

The timing worked perfectly. With the car, it would only take me five minutes to get to hers, and I still had lots of work to do. It actually felt as if, as soon as a piece of work was done, it magically duplicated to create two new tasks. Never ending cycle.

I was absorbed in an email when I noticed my phone's notification light blinking pink. Hannah's colour.

> **Hannah: leaving now**

Great. I updated my to-do list in my notebook, ready for the next day. Why were my to-do lists ever-expanding, and never ever-shrinking? I'd seen some people's to-do list that were less than five items' long. Tonight, mine was on two and a half pages of my A5 notebook. Single-spaced too.

"What're you doing?" Millie peeked over my shoulder and frowned. "You're writing a novel or something?"

"Not a novel. No, that's my to-do list for tomorrow."

Millie looked horrified.

"It's not as bad as it looks," I said, trying to justify myself and my fondness for this monstrous list. "See, everything is on there, including some stuff that might take me only a minute."

"But why put it on the list if it's only going to take a minute? Wouldn't it be quicker to do it, than to write it down?"

"Yes," I conceded, "it might be, but usually, I either discover or remember that I have to do the thing when I'm in the middle of something else, or, if I need to talk to someone face to face, when the person isn't available. So I just write it down, and then, at the end of the day, I start a fresh list, organised by order of priority, with whatever didn't get done the day before. And it's not necessarily the biggest job at the top of the list either. Here"—I pushed the notebook to the side so she could see better—"for tomorrow, I have a ton of little things at the top, because having a list that's too long stresses me out."

"But, why do you have to write it all down?" Millie's voice betrayed her confusion.

"Because not having to remember it frees up my brain space. Same reason I pack my own lunch, and I will have the same thing for lunch every day. It means it's one less decision I have to make, so I can use my brain power for more important, or more complex things."

"You have the same thing for lunch every day?"

I rolled my eyes. Here I was, trying to explain time management, productivity, and efficiency, and all she got out of that was that I ate the same lunch every day. "Only for a week," I said, "I have four lunch options in total, and I will make each option for one week, on a rota."

"Let me guess," Millie said, holding her finger up

between us as if to stop me spoiling the end of a movie. "Your rota is written down on a calendar in your kitchen so you don't have to remember whether it's sushi week or salad week."

"Pretty much." The way Millie had said it made it sound like a very strange habit, but, to me, it was efficient. I saw these indecisive people in the cafeteria at lunchtime when I popped in for my post-lunch coffee (decaf of course, because it was after twelve), and they were taking forever to choose what they wanted to eat, oohing and uhhing over the various options. Would they have a sandwich or a hot meal? But the soup of the day looked pretty good. And ooh, they had that salad they'd quite liked last time they had it.

No way was I going to waste ten minutes of my life everyday just to figure out what I was going to have for lunch. Didn't they realise that, over a year, that was nearly two whole days, forty hours, every year, trying to figure out what to have for lunch? In that daily wasted time, they could learn a new language, and be reasonably competent by the end of the year.

"Anyhoo," Millie said, "I wanted to see if you want to join us for dinner and drinks tonight?"

"Where are you guys going? Just your hotel?"

"No, I mentioned the pizza place you'd talked about to a few people, and we decided we'd try it."

My mouth watered at the thought of a spinach, artichoke's hearts, and chorizo pizza from Giuseppe's. With lots of extra chillies, and five different kinds of cheese. "What time are you guys going?" I'd committed to myself to looking up Lynn's address, and to digging into her life, and Hannah was expecting me. Although, I could drive to Hannah's and then walk to Giuseppe's.

"We booked for 6:45 p.m. We wanted later, but the guy on the phone said he was booked out."

"The place is popular week round, it's not just a weekend treat type of thing. It's quite small too, which is a shame, but when Giuseppe wanted to expand next door a few years ago, the council said no."

"Oh, that's a shame," Millie said, sounding like she really didn't care. "So, are you joining us or not?"

"Yes, I will, but I might be a few minutes late."

"That's fine, but don't complain if we've eaten all the garlic bread."

11

I managed to snag a parking spot reasonably near Hannah's and walked to her door, shoulders hunched and head tucked low against the dense drizzle. I knocked and let myself in. "Crappy weather."

Hannah appeared in the stairs, towelling off her hair. "Tell me about it," she said. "I must have left the salon at the worst possible moment, I was soaked by the time I got here, and that's not even ten minutes' away. Do you want one?" she asked holding her towel up.

I patted my hair. "Nah, I'm good, I drove, so it's only a little bit damp."

"Do you want some serum? It might frizz up otherwise?"

I stared incredulously at Hannah. "When has my hair not been frizzy, regardless of how much goop I put on it?"

Hannah looked a bit put off and I bit my lower lip. I hadn't meant to snap, but it looked like I'd hurt her feelings anyway.

"I'm sorry, that didn't come out right. I meant thank you very much for the offer, but I'm afraid it won't make a big difference. Besides, I don't have much time. A bunch of colleagues are going to Giuseppe's for dinner at 6:45 p.m., and they invited me to join."

Hannah put her fist on her hips. "You? You're going to dinner with colleagues? Who are you and what did you do with my friend Abigail?"

I chuckled. "You're right, but it's *Giuseppe's* and just the thought of his special pizza is making my mouth water. You should join us." It was an afterthought, but now I'd said it, I really did want Hanna to join us. She'd be an ally. And she was right, I hated hanging out with colleagues after work, because it felt like it was still work.

Hannah's nose formed a tiny wrinkle at the top. "I'd love to, but I'm going to my clubbing class tonight."

"Clubbing class?"

"Yeah, it's really cool, especially in the evening class, it's kind of a mix between boxercise and Zumba, but the sound is clubbing music, and we hold glowsticks, and there's a disco ball, it's so much fun," Hannah said enthusiastically, miming the punches and jabs as she talked. "You should totally join me!"

I nodded along. I was amused by the idea, really happy that Hannah had found yet another form of exercise she really enjoyed, but the idea of clubbing music, glowsticks, and Zumba were as far from my idea of fun as possible.

My fitness regimen—though it felt a bit grand calling it that—was a lot more functional, and a lot more erratic. I could go to the local boxing gym or for a (short) run three times a week for three months, then not go at all for six. The only form of exercise I'd been pretty consistent with was yoga. I'd been doing it almost every day for the past three years. It was ideal for consultant life, all I needed was a travel mat and in a pinch, I could always use a spare bath towel.

"Maybe one day," I said, "but you know I don't have much coordination, so I'm not sure I'd enjoy it." Hopefully that was a nicer way to say, 'I don't want to.' And it was true, I had zero coordination.

I pulled my laptop out and set it on Hannah's kitchen table. "So, I need to find my boss's home address, and find out as much about her life as possible. Since I don't really do social media, that's where I need your help."

"I'll put the kettle on. Why are we stalking them?" Hannah asked, busying herself with mugs and teabags.

"Remember on Monday, that threat I showed you?"

"Sure, the one with the weird symbol?"

"That's the one. Well, she called me last night, but I didn't pick up."

Hannah poured the hot water in the mugs. "Why not?"

"My phone was already on do-not-disturb for the evening. Anyway, she left a voicemail and she said she received another note, but there was something in her tone that wasn't right. And then she didn't show up for work today, and no one knew where she was."

"Hmm," Hannah said, non-committal, as she placed a steaming hot mug of tea in front of me and sat at my side. "Can I listen to the message?"

I played it for her on speaker. *Abigail, it's Lynn, call me back as soon as you get this, there was another note waiting for me when I got home.*

"Hmm," Hannah said, "She's not saying much. Did you call her back?"

"I tried, but her phone must be off, it's going straight to voicemail. That's why I wanted to find her address, I wanted to see the note." And also make sure nothing bad had happened to her.

"Not sure you'll find her home address, that's not really the kind of stuff you put online, is it?"

"No, but I was thinking her house might be visible in some of her social media pictures, and we might recognise it."

"Whoa, that's a whole new level of stalking."

"What do you mean?"

Hannah left the room, talking all the way. "Well, before I go on a date with a new guy, I check him out a bit, try to make sure he isn't too weird, or a psychopath, this sort of thing. I never even thought about figuring out where he lives based on pictures." She came back and set her own laptop on the table. "If you're that worried, why don't you just report it to the police?"

I fought the urge to undo my tight bun. Dinner with colleagues was, as far as I was concerned, still work, therefore I had to look just as neat and professional, even if it meant being bloody uncomfortable.

"Well, for starters, Lynn was very clear, she doesn't want me to involve the police. And also, what if there's nothing wrong with her, the police go to her house and she's there, completely fine? She might just have had a twenty-four-hours' stomach bug. And if that's the case, not only will I look like a complete idiot, but Lynn will make my life a living hell."

* * *

Hannah booted up her laptop and looked at me expectantly. "Right, where do we start?"

I pulled out a notepad. "You start with Facebook, I'll start with LinkedIn."

"You think she'd put her address on LinkedIn?"

"I want to look at where she's worked. When she told me about the first note, she denied knowing what it was about, but I think she did know, so it might have to do with one of her past projects."

We worked in silence, the local radio playing softly in the background.

After ten minutes of scrolling through LinkedIn, it became obvious it wouldn't lead me anywhere. Lynn's profile was pretty bare, just indicating she'd started at the consultancy straight out of uni, just like I did, and she hadn't listed each project she'd done there. Her profile picture was a professional headshot, done at least ten years ago, in my opinion.

I searched online for 'Lynn James', but that returned too many results to sift through. I added Winburyton to the key words and the results became much more manageable.

She'd been a town councillor for the last decade but I couldn't figure out why, all her votes seemed to have been designed to damage the town. Her latest one would have raised the rents in the high street by so much that it would have priced my beloved independent shops out of the centre, which in turn would have meant them going out of business. Probably no lost love there.

She'd also been named in an embezzlement case, but had been cleared of all wrongdoings. In one of the articles, there was a picture of her and her husband Elliott, dressed to the nines at a charity event at the local theatre, but they didn't say anything about him, except that he ran a successful event planning business.

"Did you find anything?" I asked Hannah who seemed deeply absorbed with her screen.

"Hmm? Oh, sorry, I got distracted. I'll go look. What did you say her name was?"

I resisted the urge to roll my eyes. I'd been told before that not everyone cared about the same things as me, that not all the things I cared about were viewed as remotely important by other people. "Lynn James."

"Let's have a look." We waited for the screen to refresh. "There are a lot of them, all over the world."

"Is there a filter of some kind?"

Hannah shook her head no.

"What if you Google her, and add Winburyton and Facebook in the key words?"

Hannah followed my suggestion, and seconds later we were back on the Facebook site, but with a much more manageable list of profiles.

"Okay, scroll down, I'll stop you if I recognise her. Hopefully she'll have her face as a profile picture."

We scrolled, but nothing came up. "Maybe she doesn't have a Facebook page," Hannah said. "After all, you don't have one," she pointed out.

"Fair enough." My brain's cogs whirred. "Try her husband, Elliott James. I just saw an article saying he had an event company, so he must have some sort of page on there."

Hannah typed. "It would be nice if his company was his name. Like Elliott James Events or something."

"It would be." I crossed my fingers, but didn't actually believe it would be the case. In the picture I'd found, Elliott was in a tux, but even without it, you could tell he was well groomed, and well educated, and my instinct told me he would have gone for something rather obscure as a company name. Maybe something in Latin.

As expected, we didn't find his Facebook profile either. "I'll Google him," Hannah said, "he must have a website under his name."

"Excellent idea."

Hannah beamed at me. "I learn from the master."

Seconds later, we'd landed on Elliott's website. As expected, his company name was weird, Spectrum Vox Events, and he appeared to be primarily organising corporate events, with a small subset of LGBTQ events, organising local Pride parades and the likes. The community was quite small, and I was surprised I hadn't heard about him, or seen the name of his company in the advertisement pages of Diva Magazine.

"Does this help?" Hannah asked

"Maybe. Scroll down to the fine print at the bottom of the page, there should be a registered office address or something, I think it's a legal requirement."

The address at the bottom of the page was local, but there was a good chance, if his business was successful, that this was an actual office, rather than his house.

I opened the map page on my browser and keyed in the address. It was in a small commercial park on the outskirts of Winburyton. Definitely not a residential address. I copied the address to my notes app. Maybe I could drive there at lunchtime tomorrow, if Lynn wasn't back. Thinking of lunch made me suddenly aware I was hungry.

I checked the clock on the laptop. "Shoot, I'm late for dinner." I packed up my stuff and wrapped Hannah in a big hug. "Thank you so much my lovely, you've been really helpful."

"Let me know if I can help more, this is kind of exciting."

12

The drizzle combined unpleasantly with the night chill and I drew my scarf higher under my chin as I left Hannah's place.

I hurried on the cobblestones, glad I hadn't decided to be fancy that morning and wear heels. It happened some days, though rarely. I would wake up and decide to wear a dress, jewellery, heels, perfume, lipstick, for no other reason than because I felt like it. I usually also craved fancy food, so made dinner with the nicest foods I could get my hands on. It was a bit like a New Year's Eve meal on any random day of the year. I called those days my flight-of-fancy days, because the whole extravaganza, while nice, was utterly impractical.

I pushed the door to Giuseppe's pizzeria open and paused on the entrance mat. I wanted to get my bearings, find where my colleagues were seated, assess the amount of people in the restaurant, noise levels, anything to remove as much unpredictability as possible.

A waiter I'd never seen before came to greet me.

"I'm meeting with some colleagues, but no idea what name they booked the table under," I said. I wasn't usually attracted to men, being quite far on the Kinsey scale, but this one was pure eye candy. From an objective point of view, he satisfied all the current canons of masculine beauty. Square jaw, glossy dark hair just the right length, a hint of stubble, symmetrical features, tall, but not freakishly so. His white shirt hung beautifully on his torso, and highlighted without clinging his well-developed muscles. I didn't need him to remove his waistcoat and shirt to guess there was a flat stomach underneath his clothes, and maybe even a hint of a six-pack.

"Do you know how many they are?" the waiter asked in smooth, barely accented English. The shiny name tag pinned on his waistcoat read, 'Marco.'

"I think they said six, so that would make seven with me."

Marco nodded. "Please follow me, we only have one party this large tonight."

I followed him to the rear of the building, doing my best to not bump into anyone. The tables were so close to each other I had to squeeze sideways between chairs. The restaurant was heaving, but that was hardly surprising. Who wouldn't want a Giuseppe's pizza on a cold and rainy autumn night?

The group was sat in the back room, one Giuseppe had sprung from what used to be the car park when the council had denied his expansion into next door.

"You came!" Millie exclaimed as I took my coat off.

Her reaction puzzled me. "I said I would, didn't I?"

She seemed confused. "Yeah, but, it was last minute, and you didn't sound too sure."

"Really?" Maybe I hadn't sounded too sure about spending time after hours with colleagues but I was most definitely sure about having Giuseppe's pizza.

At the other end of the table, an intense conversation was going on, judging by the four men's knitted eyebrows and focused faces as they listened to the fifth. I nodded at them, and asked Millie, "What's going on over there?"

"Don't know, I think they started a new topic while you and I were talking." She leaned forward. "Hey guys, what's so interesting over there?"

Anthony, who'd been talking, raised an eyebrow, as if asking for permission from the others.

"Yeah, go on, tell them, it's too juicy not to," the guys chorused.

A thin smile appeared on Anthony's face. As training lead, he was one of the people on the project who interacted with everyone, and who was in all the leadership team meetings. He usually had good intel. "So, I heard that Peter, the Finance guy?" He paused to make sure we knew who he was talking about. "Anyway, so, I heard he got fired today."

That didn't track with my conversation with Lynn and Jeff. "You mean he got kicked off the project?"

Anthony shook his head no. "No, I mean he got fired, *hasta luego, sayonara,* from the whole company."

I glanced at Millie, who seemed in shock, before returning to Anthony. "Why? How?"

"I heard, and obviously no idea if it's true, but I heard, from multiple sources, so that would suggest it's true—"

"Ant, get on with it," I said.

"Come on Abs—"

"Abigail."

He continued as if he hadn't heard me. "You know I have to put caveats, I don't want to be quoted saying it's true when it's all rumours at the moment."

"Fine," I conceded.

"Anyway, no idea if it's true, but apparently, he's been caught verbally abusing women, not just on this project, but on previous projects too. I heard his file in HR, at least if it was a paper file, would be this thick," he said spreading his thumb and index finger as far as they would go. Anthony had big hands. That would be a very thick file indeed.

I sat back while I processed. I wasn't surprised by Peter's misdeeds, since Lynn had hinted at them the day before. No, what amazed me was how efficient the R&G rumour mill was. Here we were, thousands of consultants, working all over the UK and Europe, and yet, within a few hours of a firing happening, the whole team would have heard. If only the rest of the organisation could be as effective.

"And they did nothing for all these years?" Millie had jumped in the conversation. She looked normal, but her features were a bit too even, as if she wore a wax mask.

"Slaps on the wrist and talking to, from what I heard, but nothing more than that."

"Hang on," Martin jumped in. "Didn't he get promoted in the last round? I'm sure it was in the January announcements."

Anthony nodded, revelling in the juiciness of his information. "Yep, he did."

"So, with all his history, they still promoted him?" Millie asked.

Anthony helped himself to another breadstick. "What can I say? I wasn't there, I didn't promote him. I'm just telling you what I heard."

"Makes you wonder," Martin said.

"What do you mean?" I asked.

"Yeah, like, if they protected him for so long, how many others are they still protecting?" Martin said.

"And what happened to turn the tables on him. Why now? Why today?" Anthony mused.

"The world is changing," I said before shutting my menu.

"Shall we order?" Yes, I was starving, but I also didn't want them to track Peter's firing back to me. I knew they would, especially if Millie talked.

A small part of me wondered if Lynn had tried to change things before yesterday, if she'd given Peter a warning when he landed on her project, and if that was why she'd received the threat.

<h1 style="text-align:center">13</h1>

All that were left on people's plates were crumbs, and in one case, a small mound of olives neatly piled on one side. Coffees, decafs and regulars, had been ordered, I'd leaned back in my chair, and we were all reminiscing about past projects. That was the thing. You put a group of consultants in a room, and everyone would have at least one other person from a previous project in common, and had stories to tell. The old adage of 'what happens on the project stays on the project' applied to the outside world, but didn't apply to the consultants, the people who were on the inside, who knew what it was really like.

A hand grasped my shoulder and I jumped before relaxing into a smile. "Hey Giuseppe, you've outdone yourself tonight."

Giuseppe's tanned face broke into a big smile. "Really? You liked?"

Everybody around the table broke into compliments and acclaims. "And it's all thanks to Abigail that we got to try your wonderful pizzas," Millie said, coquettish.

I smiled. She was wasting her time, Giuseppe was completely, one hundred percent, gay, with no chance of veering off track. But then again, maybe she wasn't flirting, maybe it was just her natural way of making people feel comfortable and wanted. How would I know? I was the last person to notice when someone flirted with me, and it usually required a third party to point it out for me. The rest of the time, I just assumed people were being friendly. I'd been burned in the past, assuming people were flirting, me flirting back, maybe being a bit heavy handed at it, and ending up looking like a complete idiot. No thanks.

At least with Giuseppe, it was easy. His friendliness was just that, without any underlying motive. Except maybe to entice me back in his restaurant, but that would happen anyway, his pizzas were scrumptious.

"*Cara mia,*" Giuseppe exclaimed, "let me give you a big hug to say hello." Joining the gesture to the words, he opened his arms wide and waited for me to stand and hug him back. I hesitated, but the decent thing to do was dive in. Had I been here with friends, rather than colleagues, I wouldn't have hesitated for a second, but I had a work persona, layered on top of my true self, which protected me. Colleagues only got to see the rigorous side of me, friends got to see the queen of double entendre and vulnerable side. Right now, my two worlds were colliding, and I didn't like it one bit. I stiffly hugged Giuseppe for a brief moment before releasing.

"Your pizzas are more and more delicious every time I visit," I said. And I meant it.

"*Eh,* that's because I use better and better ingredients, *cara mia,*" he said with a big smile. "I'm always looking for new suppliers you see, and every time I go to see my family in Rome, I go tasting everything." He extended his arms, punctuating each word with his hands. "The olive oil, the bresaola, the burrata, the artichokes, the tomatoes, everything. You can't make a good pizza if you don't love what you do, and that means you have to be interested in everything that goes in it, from the wheat for the flour to the type of wood you have in your oven. Everything matters, everything is important."

"I'm so glad we have you here Giuseppe," I said, touched by the passion in his monologue.

"*Cara* Abigail, I'm glad I'm here too, but I don't know if I'm going to be here for much longer," he said. The smile was still there, but it was as if a shadow had passed across his face, the corners of his eyes had tightened a little, his smile was no longer genuine, but forced.

"What do you mean?" Millie asked. "Are you going to close?"

"I hope not," Anthony said, "we've only just discovered this place, we were just talking about making this a regular weekly dinner spot for all of us."

"Err, I don't know yet," Giuseppe said, looking slightly embarrassed, as if he'd said too much and regretted it.

"What's going on Giuseppe?" I asked.

"*Eh*, you know the things of the heart are complicated. Even if you love each other . . . But we will see. I do not know the future," he said, a pained smile crossing his lips.

* * *

Driving home in the deserted streets of Winburyton, I couldn't stop thinking about Giuseppe's comment. I didn't even know he'd been seeing someone, not since his epic breakup with Ben six or seven years ago. Why hadn't he said something? Why hadn't he introduced me to his boyfriend? I saw him almost every Friday night at the Dark Horse, our local pub, and he'd never said anything. I'd ask Hannah, maybe she'd heard something?

14

Nothing like the middle of the day on a Friday to ambush someone. Or so I hoped.

I grabbed my lunch box from the shared fridge and stashed it into my messenger bag. Hopefully, talking to Elliott wouldn't take long, and I'd have time to eat before my next meeting.

Lynn still wasn't back, and Jeff wasn't in either. According to his personal assistant, he was at the head office in London dealing with the aftermath of the whole Peter mess, so asking him whether he'd heard from Lynn wasn't an option.

I hopped in the car and drove to the small commercial estate on the other side of Winburyton where Lynn's husband was supposed to have an office.

The car park, serving three dozen units, only had a few cars dotted around. I expected it was busier after four o'clock, or on weekends. I checked my phone against the map by the car park entrance. Elliott's unit was on the other side, tucked between a garage offering cheap MOTs and an artisan chocolatier.

It was a sunny day, and birds in nearby trees chirped cheerfully, so I decided to walk, rather than move the car. Besides, it would do me good to get some exercise.

Elliott's office didn't look like much from the outside. Frosted glass door, a sign labelled 'Spectrum Vox Events', and the opening hours. Afternoons were by appointment only, but I'd gotten there just in time, if the sign was right.

If Elliott had decided to go for an early lunch, I was stuffed. I tried the door, but it was locked. I rang the bell and waited. Heavenly chocolate smells wafted in from the unit next door, making my mouth water. Maybe I should go investigate there after I was done with Elliott. I wondered if they sold to members of the public. Having fresh artisan chocolate for dinner tonight sounded so good. I was about to ring the bell a second time when a silhouette appeared behind the glass and unlocked the door. The man I'd seen in the gala picture was in front of me, older, maybe late forties, casually dressed in a black turtleneck that I'd be willing to bet a pizza from Giuseppe's was cashmere, and clean, unripped and un-distressed dark blue jeans. His shoes were shiny black ankle boots.

"Elliott James?" I asked.

"Yes, how may I help you?" he asked with a bright smile.

"I work with your wife, I'm Abigail."

A shadow passed across Elliott's face. "I'm sorry, I don't think she's mentioned you . . . Would you like to come in?"

He stepped aside, holding the door open for me, and I walked into an unimpressive office. Functional, yes, with its two sofas arranged in an L, a coffee table with a jug of water and glasses, the two desks behind, a wall covered with cork- and white-boards, the other wall with a huge frame of news clippings and pictures of previous events, the shelf holding six awards arranged neatly, but overall unimpressive. No hardwood floors, but a grey short pile carpet that was probably the same in every unit, and the dreaded magnolia walls.

"Take a seat," Elliott said, indicating the sofa. "How may I help you?"

"I just wanted to know if Lynn was all right?"

Elliott cocked his head to the side. "What do you mean? Why wouldn't she be?"

I bit the inside of my cheek. What if Lynn was cheating on him and I put my foot in it?

"Err, well, she wasn't in the project office yesterday, and I've tried calling her, but her phone is going straight to voicemail, so I was wondering if maybe she was sick or something?"

"Her mother had a bad fall night before last, Lynn went to take care of her. I wasn't home, but she sent me an email really late Wednesday night." He leaned forward and poured himself a glass of water. "I guess she was in a rush when she left and she forgot to take her phone charger, or she thought she had a spare at her mother's house. I don't know."

"And you don't think it's strange she hasn't contacted you since she left?"

Elliott looked down, seemingly absorbed by a small stain on the grey carpet. "Listen, not that it's any of your business, but Lynn and I have never been a couple that's glued to each other. She was already a consultant when we met twenty-five years ago, and up until two and a half months ago, she was only home between Thursday nights and Monday mornings. It's been an adjustment for both of us." His watch beeped as a notification appeared on the screen. "If you'll excuse me, I have an appointment."

I was politely but firmly thrown out. Back in the sun, I wondered about Lynn as I walked to the car. The whole thing seemed off to me. I got Elliott's point about the adjustment, that was the main reason I hadn't even tried to have a serious relationship in years, but he really hadn't seemed that bothered.

And, even if Lynn had gone to visit her mother and forgotten her mobile charger, why wouldn't she have contacted the office? According to Elliott, she'd been gone for a day and a half. She would have had plenty of time to find a charger. Or buy one. Or find a landline and call the head office. Or send an email.

I beeped the car open and sat down, still thinking. From here, I could see Elliott's unit. Just. The sun shone through the windscreen and it was almost warm. My meeting with Elliott had been a lot shorter than expected, and I couldn't go poke around their house, since I hadn't obtained the address. Fail and fail. I pulled my lunch out of the bag. Eating in the sun in the car was still eating in the sun, and it beat eating at my desk under fluorescent lights.

I took my time, savouring every morsel, then tipped the box over my mouth to get the last grain of rice and the last drop of soy sauce. I couldn't help it. Even though it was the fifth day in a row of having the same lunch, I still loved it. I ate my apple, and checked the clock. I'd been out of the office for over an hour, I'd better get back.

I turned the key in the ignition, and a thought crossed my mind. Elliott had said he had an appointment, but no one had come in, and he hadn't gone out. Why would he lie? I chewed on it for a minute. Maybe I was overthinking. It could very well have been an online appointment, and my imagination and my love of Sherlock Holmes was getting the best of me. I wasn't a detective, and I really needed to remember it.

15

Hannah had called me as I was about to leave the office. She'd found something, but she'd refused to say what, which was why I ran out of the office as soon as my last meeting of the week was done.

"Hello?"

"In the kitchen."

Hannah's laptop was on the table, with the charging cable stretched out over a chair to a socket in the wall. An accident waiting to happen.

"Tea's ready."

I set my bag down and put my coat on the back of a chair. "So, what did you find that got you so excited?"

Tongue poking out of her lips, Hannah carried the two mugs and set them carefully on the table.

"I think it's pretty good," she said, sounding giddy.

Saying I was intrigued was putting it mildly, but I refrained from prodding, and let her talk.

"One thing I realised after you'd left was that I hadn't seen a picture of that woman you were looking for, Lynn, so I looked up her LinkedIn profile." Hannah now looked like Jasper when he'd pooped in the litter box and had sent litter flying everywhere. Really damn proud of himself. I braced myself for the worse.

"What did you do?" I asked, unable to contain the anxiety from my voice.

"Oh, nothing bad, don't worry. I just looked at her profile, it's not like I sent a message, I'm not stupid," Hannah said defensively.

I patted her hand reassuringly. Or at least I hoped it was reassuring. "I know, I'm sorry my lovely."

"I recognised her," Hannah burst out.

"You did?"

"She's a customer," Hannah said proudly.

There was something new. I'd never in a million years considered the fact that Lynn could be going to a local salon. I always pictured her as the kind of woman who'd go to a fancy salon in London and pay five hundred pounds for a cut and colour. Not go to a local place that charged a hundred and twenty quid at most.

"Does that mean you know where she lives?"

Hannah shook her head. "No, but I've got her number."

If Lynn was as worried about privacy as I was, then this was her work number, but I'd humour Hannah. She looked so proud, I didn't want to poop on her happiness. I pulled out my phone to compare Lynn's work number to the one on the paper Hannah had pushed in front of me.

My voice caught in my throat and came out slightly shaky. "They're different." I looked up. "Do you realise what this mean?"

"That I have her personal number?" Hannah said proudly.

I wrapped her in a giant hug. "It means you're bloody brilliant, that's what it means."

I started punching the digits in my phone and Hannah stopped me. "You won't tell her it was me who gave you the number, will you? I could lose my job, we're not supposed to use customer information for anything except confirming their appointments."

"Of course not." I put the phone to my ear, waiting for it to connect. A second later, Lynn's familiar voice sounded.

"Thank you for your call, I'm not available at the moment, please leave a message."

I hung up. "Straight to voicemail," I said to Hannah who looked at me expectantly. "Tell me. What do you think are the odds that a woman who went to see her mother in hospital would have forgotten the chargers for both her personal and her work phone, and who wouldn't have bought a new one for either, or both, forty-eight hours later?" Especially a woman who was as work-obsessed and controlling as Lynn.

"Zero, but what are you on about?" Hannah asked.

I told her about my visit to Elliott, and his weird reaction when I started digging into his story.

"Maybe he killed her," Hannah said wistfully.

Her words sent a chill down my spine. "Why would you say that?"

"Oh, just something Lynn told me, let's see, maybe about two or three months ago? I remember it was really hot in the salon that day. Anyway. She let it slip that she thought her husband was having an affair."

Husbands killing their wives because they had an affair was the stuff you read about in mysteries and a frequent motive for murder in TV shows, but in real life? "Why would he kill her, when he could just have asked for a divorce?"

Hannah smiled. "I've been asking around"—I shuddered—"discreetly, don't worry," she rushed to add, "and, it looks like Elliott's company isn't doing well, not well at all actually."

"That's odd, from his website it sounded like he was doing lots of corporate gigs, those must pay a lot."

"Well, I heard from Sandy, you know Sandy, curly blond hair, quite short, full of life, who works behind the counter at the bank?" I nodded. I knew Sandy, and her exuberance scared me. "She said that for the last year, Elliott has been coming in every month to transfer money from the personal joint account to his company's account."

"So Lynn is the one actually funding the company?"

"Sound like it."

"But why would he go in the branch, when he could have done it online, and no one would have noticed?"

"Sandy said their joint account require the signatures from both account holders for any transfers out of the account. So, he brings the signed transfer order in the branch."

"But in that case, wouldn't the bank want both holders to sign in front of them?"

Hannah shook her head no. "I asked Sandy about it, and apparently they got a special permission or something, years ago, after they got married, to just bring the signed form, because Lynn was always travelling. The only thing the branch does differently for them is that every year they send a statement with a list of all the transfers, and whether both parties were present or not."

"Hmm. Weird, but I guess if the bank was fine with it, it must be legal."

Hannah pointed at my empty mug. "Do you want another one?"

"Better not, I need to go home to feed Jasper."

While it was technically true, it was also the perfect excuse to leave and satisfy the craving to be on my own. I loved Hannah to bits, so it really wasn't about her, but I just wanted to close the door on an empty apartment, grab whatever was in the fridge and in the cupboards that didn't require using the hob, and flop on the sofa while watching whatever TV boxset I had waiting in my Netflix queue.

I pointed at the papers on the table. "What are these?"

"Printouts from Companies House, showing that the company isn't doing that well, and that Lynn is a co-director."

"How do you know the company isn't doing well?"

"Well, I'm no accountant, but when the company's profits are negative every year, I'm guessing it's not good?"

I was astonished. "And you found that online?"

"Yep, it's all there, all publicly available, you just need to know the name of the company and you're in business."

"Huh." I was speechless. Hannah was a much, much better detective than I was. And while I loved my friend, I was also, in this moment, extremely envious of her. Regardless of how smart I thought I was, she was clearly smarter.

* * *

"What gave you the idea of looking at Companies House?"

Hannah's cheeks took a pink tinge and she lowered her eyes. "You're going to laugh at me."

I held both hands up. "I absolutely one hundred percent promise I will not laugh."

"There's this author I like, she writes love stories, romance, but there's always an element of the women bettering themselves, without help, and they just happen to find love along the way, and anyway, in one of her books, the heroine starts a business, and she calls Companies House to register it."

"Wow, Hannah." I had to say something nice to her, something complimentary, that hopefully wouldn't show how envious I was. "I never would have thought about it, you're brilliant."

"Not as much as you," Hannah said, "you have a really fancy job."

"I'm starting to realise my fancy job really doesn't matter. You're the brilliant one," I insisted. I pulled the pages from Hannah's hands. "And is that why you went to see Sandy?"

"Yeah . . . I wasn't sure what any of it meant, and she explained some of it. Did you know she's doing an online course to become an accountant?"

"I didn't, but good for her." I pushed my chair back and started pacing around the kitchen. Movement helped me think. "Did Sandy say when the next annual statement was due to be sent?"

"No, why? Is it important?"

My pacing was more two steps forward and two steps back, owing to the size of Hannah's kitchen, but the juices were flowing anyway. "What if Elliott's been forging his wife's signature on the transfer authorisations? And he's been getting away with it too, but the bank is about to send the next statement. He panics, of course. Everyone is scared of Lynn—"

"Except you," Hannah pointed out.

Was I or wasn't I? What did scare me? Spiders, although it wasn't a phobia, I was fine with them outside, I just didn't want them in my flat. My favourite brand of bras going out of business was also scary. Not having a source of income was also really high on my fears' list, but that was probably the same for everybody.

"No," I said slowly, "I think a part of me *is* scared. Not of her as a person, but of her power. She could have me fired just like she's had Peter fired, and I would be homeless."

Hannah's brow furrowed. "How'd you work that out?"

"No job means no flat."

Hannah drew herself as tall as her five feet two allowed. "I'd smack you if I could."

I lowered myself in the chair. "Can we not talk about this please? I was already feeling a bit flat before coming over, but this is just depressing."

"No!" Hannah drew her chair closer to mine and took my hands in hers. "You, my dear friend, will not be homeless."

I knew Hannah meant well, but I really didn't want to have this conversation, not when my batteries were close to empty. And probably not on full batteries either.

"I know you, I know you have savings, and remember when you were saving up for a deposit? You're a pro with all the cutting on spending," she said. "And if you had to, you could always get a lodger, that would help with the mortgage."

I shuddered at the idea of having someone living with me, but Hannah had made her point. "Thank you my lovely, you're a good friend."

Hannah frowned. "How did we get on to that topic?"

I replayed the train of thoughts in reverse until I hit the last relevant point. "Elliott was scared of Lynn, just like everyone else."

"So you think he killed her because he didn't want to explain the transfers from the joint account to his company?"

"I don't know. We don't even know she's dead, Elliott might have told the truth, and she might simply be visiting her mother."

As I put my coat on, I wondered. Had Elliott told the truth? Would Lynn waltz in the office on Monday as if nothing had happened?

16

Another email pinged in my inbox and I fought the urge to scream. Would this craziness ever stop? Not even eleven and the day had gone completely pear-shaped. From the moment I got in just after seven to now, I'd been running around the office and hopping from video call to video call, fixing crisis after crisis.

Mondays were never usually that busy, what with us—the onsite consultants—trickling into the office from all over the country—and in some cases, Europe—it meant we couldn't really have meetings in the morning, but today . . . Was it a full moon or something?

I took a deep breath, willing the world to slow down, even if only for five minutes, so I could regroup. My lips were so dry from dehydration they'd cracked and were bleeding in several places. How bad was it that I hadn't even had time to take a sip of water throughout the morning?

Millie shuffled next to me, looking guilty.

"Oh, what now?" I asked. "What did you break? Which of my stakeholders had a meltdown? Who's no longer understanding the plan?" I just wanted five minutes of peace and quiet, was that too much to ask?

"None of the above," Millie said. "I noticed you seemed to be having a tough morning, so I brought you this." She laid a napkin on my desk and drew a perfectly iced cupcake from behind her back. I looked from the cupcake to her face and back, speechless.

"Thank you," I eventually managed. "But why?" In my experience, people were never nice just because, they always wanted something from you, they always had an ulterior motive.

Millie looked away. "I was just trying to be nice," she muttered.

"Nice? To me?" No one ever wanted to be nice to me unless they wanted something. I wasn't a nice person in general. People usually wanted to avoid me. "Why?"

"I just want you to like me, is that so bad?" she whispered.

"But why? You seem reasonably competent at your job, and as long as you're not creating more work for me, we're good. I don't need to like you, you don't need to bring me cupcakes."

Millie's eyes filled with tears and she walked away. I felt a pang of guilt in my chest, I must have said or done something wrong, but what? I'd said thank you. I'd explained she didn't need to bring me food. I didn't understand her reaction.

I dipped the tip of my little finger into the cupcake icing and tasted it. Hmm, buttercream, my favourite. So much better than cream cheese.

I was about to text Hannah to share my incomprehension when I saw her message.

> Hannah: have u seen the news
> Me: No, why?
> Hannah: check winburyton chronicle
> website!!!

It wasn't like Hannah to be so mysterious. And three exclamation marks? Punctuation of any kind was unheard of in her texts.

I opened a new tab in the browser and duly searched for our local newspaper. What could be that exciting in the local news? I felt a pang of anxiety. What if Giuseppe's was closing?

The website loaded, and I didn't need to ask Hannah what it was she wanted me to see. Filling the screen almost completely was a picture of the town centre park, people around the edges and uniformed police constables in the middle, a blue-and-white barrier tape dividing the two. Below the picture, the headline screamed at me.

WOMAN'S BODY FOUND IN PARK POND

I clicked on the link, and, after a nail-biting wait, the page eventually loaded. No surprise there, the whole of Winburyton must have been trying to view the same article as me.

The journalist had obviously written his copy fast, and hadn't taken the time (or bothered) to run it past the proof-reader. He also didn't provide much information, since the police hadn't released any.

In essence, a woman had been found dead by an elderly gentleman who'd come to feed the ducks. The woman's name wouldn't be released until her family had been notified. The police was treating the death as suspicious. The elderly gentleman was being treated for shock.

That was it. No indication of the woman's age, or how long she'd been dead for.

Me: No reason to jump to conclusion. It
could be anyone.

Hannah: OMG are you serious it has to
be her

I shut the screen. Neither one of us had any real information, no point in going through the loop of 'it's her' - 'it could be anyone.'

The cupcake on my desk was making me feel guilty, but I didn't know what to do about it. I opened the phone again.

Me: Millie brought me a cupcake.

Hannah: buttercream or cream cheese

Me: Buttercream.

Hannah: any reason

Me: She said she noticed I was busy.

Hannah: OMG she likes you

Me: Yes, she said so. She also said she
wanted me to like her.

Hannah: no likes you LIKES you

Huh? How did Hannah figure that one? Since when did cupcake-bringing automatically equate to romantic intent? Was bringing a cupcake the modern equivalent to giving a knight your sleeve in the Middle Ages? Was a cupcake-offering a marriage proposal? Why was the world of humans so complicated? The more I stared at the cupcake, the more my head hurt.

"You know, you're supposed to eat it, not try to hypnotise it."

I jumped at the gently mocking voice behind me. "Jeff, don't scare me like that! I wasn't trying to hypnotise it, I was trying to figure out what it meant."

Jeff raised an eyebrow. "It's a cupcake. You eat it. It makes your brain feel happy, for a little bit. That's it. Do you have five minutes?"

I nodded, speechless. Was life really that simple in other people's brains?

"Come on, let's find a room."

I grabbed my notebook and wordlessly followed Jeff in the elusive search for a free meeting room. These were akin to the Loch Ness monster. You'd heard reports they existed, but could never seem to find one when you went looking.

We found a tiny one in another part of the building, one we, project people, were not supposed to use, since they were reserved for the client's sales team, but Jeff marched in the room, barely bigger than a booth, and took a chair. I took the other one and waited for him to talk. If I was in trouble, I'd rather he told me what for, than me volunteering options.

"You're not in trouble, don't worry." Wait what? Was the man a mind-reader? "No need to look so surprised, the death grip you've got on your notebook is a dead giveaway." His face darkened. "I heard from Lynn's husband. Apparently, her mother is unwell, and she had to go there in a hurry. It sounded like she isn't going to be coming back for a while, so we need to make sure her work is covered."

"Okay . . ." Why was he telling *me* this?

"That's where you come in." Damn him and his mind-reading powers. "I remember you from the Assare project, must be coming on eight years ago now, you were still green, yet you were miles ahead of your peers. That hasn't changed, except you're a lot less green."

I narrowed my eyes. Was he implying I was old? I was

barely over thirty, thank you very much, whereas he was at least fifty. Ancient. "Okay . . ."

"I want you to step up and take on Lynn's role, at least until she's back."

What?

"I'm sorry Jeff, can you repeat that please, I don't think I heard you correctly." Also known as *what?!*

"I want you, Abigail Palmer, to take on the project manager role formerly fulfilled by Lynn James, until said Lynn James comes back from looking after her mother." Jeff's eyes twinkled as he spoke. The bastard was enjoying this. He knew the opportunity was too good for me to pass on, and he also knew I hated those types of roles because they were all about people management. Bleurgh.

"What about *my* role? You know I'm one of the best in this area. How are you going to find a replacement senior Sales module functional consultant, who also happens to be an experienced team lead, at such short notice? We can't lose even one day of work, or the whole workstream is going to concertina and come crashing against the go-live date. It's going to be a train wreck."

Jeff smiled. "I know all that. And you're already speaking like a project manager, so you're taking the role. I already spoke to your line manager, he's happy for you to do both roles."

My heartbeat had accelerated so much I thought I would need a defibrillator. "Both roles? Are you crazy? No one can do both at the same time."

Jeff looked at me, his eyes now devoid of any malice or mockery. "You can. You don't see it, I know that, but I've seen you juggle more, successfully, than consultants with triple your experience. You can do this."

"Can I at least think about it?" This was too much for

one person, I knew it. There was no way this would work. "And what if people accuse me of bias against my own workstream? And how am I supposed to deal with all the admin? It's too much for one person."

Jeff smiled. He obviously thought he'd won the battle. "We'll give you a PMO person to help with the reporting, and keeping on top of the trackers, for the Sales workstream. As PM, you'll have the full PMO team at your disposal, minus that one person."

"But I'm really bad with people, you know that as well as I do. Maybe better even, I know people complain about me."

"You'll be great, just be yourself. Oh, and if you want to date Millie, you can, just keep it quiet. I don't want the client or the rest of the team to hear about it."

My jaw dropped. "What? How . . .?"

Jeff chuckled. "Come on Abigail . . . she brought you a cupcake!"

17

I'd been turning Jeff's offer (or maybe I should have said 'order') in my head all afternoon, and I wasn't any closer to a decision.

After what had happened with Peter, I seriously doubted my abilities to manage a team of (officially) forty-five people, especially when at least seventy percent were older than me, with a lot more experience than me. And while the project manager didn't officially manage the client's people, in reality, they kind of did, effectively doubling the size of the team I was supposed to manage.

Not to mention having to go to all the steering committee meetings with all the big cheeses in the client's company. How could I spin so many plates? What if I dropped one? Would people point and laugh, like they did when I'd dropped my lunch tray at school? And what should I do about Millie? Did I want to date her? Was I attracted to her? One thing I was certain of was that I *shouldn't* date her just because she wanted to date me. That was a recipe for disaster. Were we even viable, long term? Or even short term? As project manager, I'd effectively be her boss. Dating in the workplace rarely ended well, what if she couldn't handle a breakup? What if *I* couldn't? Would we get sick of each other?

I pulled my phone out and texted Hannah.

Me: Too many thoughts, head's spinning.

I straightened in my chair and tried to do breathing exercises while I waited for her to reply.

How was I supposed to handle the job if just the thought of it, before I even started doing it, sent me into a tailspin?

No response from Hannah. If she was with a customer, it could be a while before she answered. An idea popped into my head and I dialled the hairdressers. Becky, the cute—and unfortunately very straight—receptionist picked up. Two minutes later, I had an appointment with Hannah.

This was exactly what I needed. A good chat, and a head massage to die for.

18

The salon was tucked away on the side of the high street, not that far away from where they'd found the woman's body. It had an old-fashioned look to it, U-shaped with the next building, their entrances facing each other under a shared ceiling. Right now, it didn't matter, but it was always good when it was raining, as it gave you a chance to open your umbrella when you left the salon before you stepped out in the rain and ruined your new do.

Through the two shopfront windows forming two walls of the salon, I could see a flurry of activity, and a couple of people waiting for their appointments. I had no desire to share a sofa with random people, especially when that sofa was on the small side. Sure, I could have waited standing, but the space wasn't designed for that, and standing meant being in everybody's way, clients leaving, stylists confirming appointments, even the young girl who swept the hair off the floor. Hannah was nowhere near done, as she'd only just started blow-drying the woman's very long hair, so I crossed the street and headed for Black's.

I didn't need cheese as such, but then again, whoever did? And maybe I could get Frank to tell me who else had the stylised-sun tattoo. Besides, cheese was good for the nerves, at least in my world.

I pushed Jeff and his take-this-job-or-else to a dark

corner of my brain, turned on the recording app on my phone, waved at Frank through the window, and pushed the door open.

"I didn't expect to see you again so soon," Frank said with an obviously fake-delighted smile plastered on his face.

"And I didn't expect you to still be open past five on a Monday," I replied in an equally (I hoped) fake-happy tone. "How come?"

"Had to close for a couple hours midday, thought I'd open a bit later to make up for it. It's all on my social media," Frank said. "What can I get you? I'm going to be closing right after you."

"I won't be long, I've got a hair appointment in a minute. They're running a bit behind, so I figured, why not get a couple of new cheeses from my favourite cheesemonger?"

"Ha, flattery will get you everywhere. Anything specific in mind?"

"I was thinking a nice ash-covered goat's cheese, but maybe also something with a bit more character?"

"Character huh?" Frank scratched his nascent beard. "How about this Basque Idiazabal?"

"Can I try some?"

Frank used his trusted cheese iron to drill into the wheel and extract a carrot-like sample. It was different. Smoky, with a spicy aftertaste. I could see it working very well with walnut bread. "I'll take a small wedge please, a couple hundred grams?"

Frank set to cutting and weighing.

"Say Frank, you know that story you told me about your tattoo the other day, the one on your arm that looks like a sun?"

Frank smiled. "Good times."

"Are you still in touch with the other guys who got the same one that night?"

"Who said it was night?" He laughed. "Nah, we were done before five."

I did my best to widen my eyes in what would hopefully look like true admiration. "Wow, that's impressive."

"Yeah, well, we were younger back then. Wouldn't be able to do it anymore. But yeah, we still see each other, not as often as we used to, but we try to meet up at the pub at least once a week, plus, for the football, rugby, birthdays, this sort of things."

I nodded, hoping he would go on.

Frank didn't disappoint. He showed me his fingers crossed. "We were like this the six of us. Sam, Leo, Aaron, Giuseppe, and Nick."

"I didn't realise Giuseppe had been living here for that long."

Frank put his fist on his waist in mock anger. "Hey, how old do you think I am?"

"Sorry, I didn't mean that, of course. I meant I thought Giuseppe had moved here about ten years ago." I took the cheese he handed me and paid.

"Nah, that's just when he opened the pizzeria. He moved here from Italy our last year of A-Levels, so 'bout thirty years now I guess?"

"Good for him. Right Frank, it was lovely to see you as ever, but I need to run."

I now had the first names of the other men branded with the same mark that was on the threat note. All I had to do was find out their last names, and their connection to Lynn. Easy right?

19

I pushed the door of the salon open, jingling the little bell above the door at the same time. Hairdryers were roaring in the small space, but its warmth, after the cold and damp outside, was comforting. Hannah had disappeared, so I sat on the now-empty sofa, observing the hairdressers' skills. One was painting on smelly goop that would later reveal beautiful highlights and lowlights, all perfectly placed to appear completely natural, one was fearlessly chopping a teenager's waist-length hair into a stylish bob, another was having a chat with an elderly customer who seemed set on having a trendy colour put on her snow-white hair. I knew from listening to Hannah that the salon was treacherous and full of politics, but as an outsider, it felt smooth, well organised, and easy. No one was having a crisis. If someone made a mistake, it wouldn't cost hundreds of thousands of pounds to put right. No one had disappeared and left me in charge when I didn't know what I was doing.

"Abigail?"

I looked up, and Hannah was in front of me. How she'd done that would remain a mystery, the girl had ninja skills. Or I'd been so lost in my thoughts I'd become oblivious to the mundane. That was a very serious possibility I had to consider.

"What are you doing here?" Hannah asked.

"I have an appointment," I said, "with you."

Hannah processed the information for a full minute, with only the whirring of the hairdryers and the low humming of voices between us. "Oh dear. What happened?"

I opened my mouth to protest and closed it again. Over time, Hannah had somehow managed to uncover the real 'me', the 'me' I took great pains to hide from the world.

"I'll trade you my story for an extra-long scalp massage," I said.

Hannah took a black gown from a rack and handed me a coat hanger. "Come on, take your coat off."

She led me to an empty chair, swivelled it so I faced the mirror, and undid my low bun. She raked her fingers through my hair for a minute. "Hmm. So, what do you want to do with it? Just a trim, as usual?"

I looked at my reflection. She was right. I always had *just a trim*. My brown hair was reasonably long, just past my shoulders, and I never did anything to it except brushing it and tying it in a low bun at the nape of my neck. At the weekend, I didn't even bother with the brushing part, I just flipped my head upside down, raked my fingers through my hair, and gathered it all in a topknot. Surprisingly, it usually looked very tidy.

"What if . . . what if you cut more?"

Hannah's eyes widened. "Are you sure?" I wasn't. Really not. "Abigail?" I met her eyes in the mirror. "What's going on?"

"I sort of got promoted." It had come out in a grumble, without the slightest twinge of excitement or optimism. If my words had been the sky, it would have been gloomy and overcast.

"That's good news, no? You don't sound too happy about it."

"It's Lynn's job."

Hannah sat on the stool next to me. "You're kidding?"

"I wish. And that's not the worst."

"It isn't?"

"They want me to do both her job *and* mine."

"That's bonkers. Your job is enough to keep a normal person crazy busy. I know you're not quite normal, but still, that's too much, even for you."

I rubbed my forehead with my palms. "Normal is boring, but right now, I think I'd rather have boring than what's coming my way."

Hannah stood up. "My boss is giving me the evil eye. Come on, let's talk hair. How about we cut four inches?"

My eyes widened when I looked at where Hannah's hand had landed. I couldn't remember having hair this short in my life. "That's a lot. Would I even still be able to tie it up? I can't have my hair down at work."

Hannah's nose wrinkled. "Why not?"

"I think it looks unprofessional. And it gets in my face when I'm typing, or eating. And it only looks good in my bathroom. The minute I step out of the house it looks messy and unkempt—"

Hannah held her hands up to stop me. "Alright, enough, I got it. No to a bob. I've got another idea."

I winced. Mostly because I was afraid that Hannah's idea would be beyond outlandish, and I would have to shoot her down again.

She took a big plastic box of sectioning clips out of a drawer and started pinning my hair. After several long and painful minutes where she tugged and folded my hair, Hannah took a step back, smoothed a rebel strand, and smiled. "What do you think?"

I stared in the mirror, speechless.

"Obviously, it's just a mock-up," Hannah said hurriedly. "It would look different properly cut, slicker."

I blinked. "I have cheekbones. You gave me cheekbones." I wasn't looking at myself anymore. Instead, the woman in the mirror sported a foxy pixie cut that made her eyes huge and gave her cheekbones that could have cut glass. The woman in the mirror looked incredible. I looked up to meet Hannah's eyes and the woman looked up too.

* * *

"So." Hannah shuffled from one foot to the other and buried her hands deep in her apron's pockets, clearly uncomfortable. "Do you like it?"

I did like it, but this was so short. What if I didn't like it anymore tomorrow? It would take forever to grow out. "I do, but I'm really not sure. That's a lot of commitment."

"And you don't do commitment, I know. It's a commitment to me too. I'll need to give you a trim every four weeks or so."

"How often?!" I was shocked. At the moment, I got the split ends trimmed twice a year, and only because Hannah insisted. I would have been happy with getting a trim only once a year. Or never.

"Obviously it depends how fast your hair grows, could be every three weeks, or you might get away with every six weeks." She cocked her head to the side. "Either way, it's a lot more than what you're used to."

I closed my eyes. I knew what I wanted to do, but the sensible side of me was still screaming that I couldn't handle such a sophisticated haircut requiring so much maintenance. A brief fight ensued in my head, until one of the parties got quashed. During the whole time, Hannah had waited quietly for me to make up my mind.

"Do it," I said in a whisper.

Hannah gathered the hair at the nape of my neck, and rested the scissors at the base of the ponytail. "Sure?"

"No, but do it anyway."

I closed my eyes and felt the blades hacking at the mass of hair, and then it was over. I cautiously peeked through my eyelashes and my gaze landed on Hannah's hand. She was proudly holding what had been my hair and now looked like Jasper's tail on a bad day. I was left with a deeply uneven bob.

"Now what?" I asked.

"Now we wash your hair and you finally start relaxing."

I let Hannah lead me to the sink by the elbow, sleepwalking through the salon as the enormity hit me. What had I done? And the worst part was that it was too late to back out. Two thirds of my hair was in the bin by Hannah's workstation. I supposed hair extensions would be an option, but probably not with my own hair. And there would be upkeep too. Hannah gently but firmly pulled my shoulders back.

"Why are you so tense? I swear you're just sitting here as if you're waiting to be called away, when most people sit and melt back in the chair."

I let her guide me back against sink. "Sorry," I muttered.

"Relax," she ordered as she turned on the water.

A few minutes later, after the usual 'too hot, too cold' exchange to get the temperature just right for me, Hannah set to working on my scalp, and slowly my stress melted away.

I was as close to asleep as I'll ever be in public when Hannah nudged me. "Come one, we're going back to the chair, it's time to transform you."

I blinked my eyes open and sluggishly followed her. This had felt so good, I wondered if they offered scalp massages on their own. I'd do it regularly. Much more regularly than getting my hair trimmed, which was always a hassle.

The station next to Hannah's was now occupied. Shruti, who had joined the local police force as soon as we were done with A-levels, hugged me. "Abigail, hi, it's been ages, how are you?"

I gingerly hugged her back, not wanting to drip on her too much. "I'm good thanks, how are you?"

"Hey, you know, busy busy."

"The usual then?"

Shruti's face got serious. "Actually, busier than usual," she said in a much lower voice, so low I could barely hear her over the sound of the hairdryers.

The dead woman in the pond, of course. "Have you identified the woman yet?"

"Abigail, come on, you know I can't tell you that."

"I'm not asking for her name, I'm only asking if you know who she is."

Shruti pressed my hand. "Sorry sweetie, I really can't tell you."

Her stylist reappeared at her side and I nodded at him. "Hi Mark. Shruti, it was a pleasure, as usual, but since you're not going to talk, I better get back to my cut."

Shruti chuckled. "You mean your life-changing new do, I think? That's looking mighty short sweetie."

Hannah returned with a cup of tea for both of us. "It's going to be a lot shorter, I'm giving her a pixie."

Shruti's hand flew to her mouth as she looked horrified. "Oh my god, really? Are you sure?"

I grimaced. "Bit too late to back out now, isn't it?"

"I suppose it is, yes. I'm sure you'll look amazing." Shruti's tone suggested otherwise.

"Back to us," Hannah said, taking me by the shoulders and putting me firmly into the chair. "Do not move, do not turn your head. If I miss, I'll have to cut even shorter, and there's going to be a point where you end up with a buzzcut."

I shuddered at the thought. I wasn't too sure about the pixie, but I knew I'd look horrible with a buzzcut. The only women I'd seen pull it off successfully were Kristen Stewart and Natalie Portman, and they'd been paid millions to do it. I, on the other hand, would be paying for the privilege.

* * *

After several minutes of careful snipping (including the top of my ear at one point), Hannah broke the silence. "So. How come you got Lynn's job? Not that you're not competent or anything, but what's the deal?"

I made to shrug and stopped myself. No moving, Hannah had said. "It's all a bit of a blur if I'm honest. Jeff said Elliott, Lynn's husband, had called him to say she was going to be gone a while. So Jeff had to find a replacement, and he picked me of all people."

"Hmm. I suppose if Elliott called in, then she must be at her mum's," Hannah said.

I sighed. None of it made sense. "I know. I was so sure though. I mean, what about the threat she'd received?

Hannah cleared her throat. I met her eyes in the mirror and she glanced over at Shruti who seemed deep in conversation with her stylist.

"It's fine," I said. I was almost certain she wasn't eaves-dropping. And what if she were? If Lynn was fine and did come back, she would be mad at me for the police being involved, even though I hadn't told them. And if Lynn wasn't fine, wasn't it better that the police knew about the threat? Although, in all fairness, the threat didn't seem like much of one anymore. 'Tell the truth or I will,' that wasn't that big a deal. It had potential for embarrassment, but that was it. I was almost certain there was nothing illegal in Lynn's past that would land her in prison. And if there was, then maybe she *should* land in prison.

Hannah straightened my head. "Let's assume she didn't call Elliott, or send him an email or anything. Why would he make it up and call the office?"

"To cover his ass?"

"I suppose, but why would he want to harm her?"

"Maybe she was cheating on him? That would explain the note. The 'tell the truth' bit would be about telling her husband she was having an affair, or her lover would."

Hannah put down her scissors for a minute to assess her progress. "That would actually make sense."

"Let's go back to the job. I haven't technically agreed to do it, but Jeff seemed to think it was a done deal."

"What happens if you say no?"

I tried to run through the potential scenarios in my head. I wouldn't get fired, but I might get kicked off the project, and end up in Siberia for the rest of my career. Siberia were the worst projects, those that had a high consultant turnover because no one wanted to be on them for longer than three months.

Those projects were always miles away from home, the client treated us as their lackeys, and, given that they paid for the service, they assumed that our bodies and souls were part of the deal too. Typically, the client also had unrealistic expectations regarding the timeline, budget, and slash or technical feasibility, they had the bad habit of changing their minds every five minutes, and to top it all, the business people were often unavailable or incompetent.

I had done of few of those projects, usually to fill in a gap between two consultants, and I'd hated every minute of it. If they did exile me to Siberia, and I decided to resign, then they could put the word out to all the other consultancies that I was 'difficult' to work with. That meant no other consultancy would touch me with a ten-foot pole, even if they were desperate for someone with my level of expertise. Maybe I could go out on my own, pick up freelance contracts. I'd need to seriously build up my savings before I could do that, who knew how long it would be before I would get my first contract?

What would happen if I said 'no'? Hannah's question rang in my head as I thought through all the potential scenarios.

"Legally, nothing. If they decided to fire me, I could sue them, because what they're asking me to do is unrealistic. No one can do those two jobs at the same time correctly, not even me. Especially not me. The thing is, I kind of want to try, it's a terrific opportunity, but I'm terrified I'll screw up."

"Terrified or not, it sounds like you're going to do it anyway," Hannah said, "so you're going to seriously plan your time—"

"I already do that, you know it, I'm the queen of lists."

"I meant plan your non-working time too. Schedule time off, schedule time for yourself, schedule time for your haircuts," she said as she tugged gently at my hair. "And for your friends. You need people who'll notice if things get too intense. And you need to have a talk with your boss, this Jeff guy." Hannah swivelled my chair a quarter turn before sitting on the stool and flipping a chunk of hair to the front. I wondered what kind of fringe she was about to cut, given the thickness of the hair curtain in front of me.

"What kind of talk?" I asked.

"The kind where you put a time limit on the arrangement. You need to put him on the clock, because if he's right and you *can* do both jobs, why would he bother finding a replacement?"

"But he thinks Lynn is coming back, so he's not going to bother finding someone else. I think, in his head, I'm doing the job until she comes back?"

"And what if she's away for six months? Or what if your original assumption is right, and she's not in a state to ever come back."

"I didn't make that assumption," I pointed out, "you did. You jumped to the conclusion that the dead woman in the pond was Lynn."

"Whatever. I'm saying you need to put him on the clock. What happens with Lynn is irrelevant. He's got three weeks max to find a permanent replacement."

I thought about it. What she'd said was sensible, but how was I supposed to have that conversation? I was aware that no one my age or level of experience ever got given that kind of opportunity. Jeff wasn't just giving me a career step stool, he was giving me a bloody trampoline.

"Maybe I should ask for more money," I mused.

Hannah was done cutting the fringe bit. I hoped it looked okay. She looked unhappy. "Abigail, it's not all about the money. What about your health? You need to look after yourself."

"I am," I insisted. "I've been thinking"—granted, only for the last five minutes, but I had been thinking about it

—"I've been thinking, maybe I should look at going freelance. It would give me control on which projects I go to, so go to the good ones, avoid the bad ones, and control on location too. I could pick projects that were local only, so I could go home every night. Or maybe even remote projects, where I could work from home and have zero commute."

"That all sounds very good, but why do you need more money now?"

"It might be a while before I get my first contract, so I need to have money saved up."

"But why?"

"From what I've heard, for freelance contracts, you get a recruiter calling you on a Tuesday for an interview on Wednesday or Thursday to start on the Monday. I'm on three months' notice at the consultancy, so I need to quit first, then, towards the end of my notice period, start looking for my first contract.

"From the moment I start looking to the moment I find one could be months. I need to make sure I can afford all the basics, like mortgage payments, and food, and regular trims for my new fancy haircut," I added pointing at my head.

"Got it. Put your head down," Hannah said as she pushed my head, giving me a nice neck stretch at the same time. "Now, don't panic, I'm just going to use the clippers to clean up the back, but don't sneeze or you'll get a reverse mohawk."

I gritted my teeth. As soon as she'd said I shouldn't sneeze, my nose started itching. The clippers vibrated against the base of my skull for a few seconds before stopping.

"Okay, I'm going to dry it now."

"Can I look yet," I whined.

"Not until it's dry. I'm going to put some serum on first."

Hannah looked around her caddy for the elusive bottle. "Bugger, someone's nicked it again. Hold on, I'll get a new one in the back. No peeking," she added as she walked away.

Curiosity was raging inside of me, but she trusted me. Hannah wanted to see my face when I discovered her creation, and the least I could do was give her this small pleasure.

"It looks great, don't worry," Shruti whispered. She was done, by the looks of it, her hair only a little shorter than it had been when she'd arrived, just . . . tidier. Why was she still here though, if she was done? She was out of her gown, and she had her coat in her arms, so she must have paid already.

"Thanks." I suspected Hannah had been right, and she had been eavesdropping. Now she wanted to question me, but I wasn't about to make it easy for her. I usually liked Shruti, but I didn't like her manipulative streak. I wondered if it was a trait she'd acquired when she'd become a detective, or if she'd always been like that.

"The woman you were talking about with Hannah, Lynn, was it Lynn James?"

"Yes, why, do you know her?"

Shruti looked over my shoulder and I followed her gaze. Hannah had reappeared, bottle in hand.

"This isn't the best place to talk." Shruti pressed a business card in my hand. "Call me tomorrow, will you, then we can arrange to meet at the police station." She left precipitately, not before calling goodbye to Hannah and the rest of the still busy salon.

"What was that about?" Hannah asked.

I looked at the business card and pocketed it. "I don't know."

20

Mid-morning break, my first morning of doing both my job and Lynn's, and it felt like I'd done a whole day's work *and* ran a marathon. Or at least I assumed that's how one felt after running a marathon. I'd never run one. Not even attempted. I'd occasionally persuaded myself to be more active, went for a run around the block of flats where I lived, then went back home as soon as I'd completed the first lap, red faced and panting.

I stood in the middle of the car park, away from prying ears, and called Shruti. She picked up on the second ring.

"Detective Sergeant Shruti Anand."

"Shruti, hi, it's Abigail."

"Oh, hi, thanks for calling. How's your new haircut?"

"It's fabulous." And I meant it. Not even the ten minutes it had taken me that morning with a hairdryer and a round brush to get the fringe to sit right detracted from that statement. Or the hair product. I'd had to buy wax. Kind of like gel, but pastier. Apparently it had been around for decades. I was a thirty-year-old woman who was discovering the world of hair products. There were a lot. The mind boggled as to why there were so many. "Hannah really outdid herself on this one."

"I'm glad it turned out well. Listen, sorry to cut the pleasantries short, but I need to run out in a sec. When can you come by the police station?"

I'd had a look at my calendar before leaving my desk, and I hoped no one had sent more meetings in the five minutes I'd been away. "I'm only really free after 4:45 p.m. Does that work?"

I heard her mouse clicking in the background. "It works."

And now that the business was concluded, as usual, I had no idea how to hang up without sounding rude. "Okay then, I'll see you at the station."

"You don't want to know what it's about?"

I rolled my eyes. "It doesn't take a genius to know it's about Lynn James. Or am I wrong?" There was silence on the other side of the line, as if we'd been cut off. "Hello? Hello?"

"Yes, I'm still here. And no, you're not wrong, but we can talk about how you figured it out later."

I hung up and rolled my eyes again. How had I figured it out. She'd asked me if I'd been talking about Lynn James, and then she'd asked me to call her. Duh.

I added a reminder in my phone's calendar and texted Hannah.

> **Me: Meeting Shruti at the station at 4.45 tonight.**
>
> **Hannah: want to come over after**

I thought about it. I debated. I didn't know how I'd feel after answering Shruti's questions. If I wanted to be alone, and I'd already committed to Hannah, then I'd feel bad about cancelling on her, and she'd be hurt. It was also possible the questioning would last for longer than ten minutes.

> **Me: Probably best not, not sure how long it's going to take, and I have a feeling I'll be peopled out afterwards.**

Hannah: np hows the new job

Me: Like I did a week's worth in the first quarter of the day.

Hannah: (((hugs))) xxx

Bless her. I finished crossing the car park to the cafeteria, made myself two cappuccinos, one extra hot, and headed back to my new desk. I was still waiting on IT to give me access to Lynn's emails and calendar, and at the moment, I was relying on Sybil, the lovely PMO girl who had the patience of an angel and the discipline of an army sergeant, to tell me which meeting I was supposed to go to, who with, and what I needed to prepare. I'd also put her in charge of going through my own calendar and move any conflicting meetings. Honestly, the woman was a saviour, and the work I'd given her was way below her.

I sat down, sipping on the regular-hot coffee, and scanned through my emails. Nothing that couldn't be delegated or wait, so far so good.

I opened our shared project plan online and hurray, it looked like Lynn's permissions had been transferred over, I finally had an all-access pass to the plan, down to level four and all the nitty-gritty details.

"Hey Sybil, do you have a sec," I called over.

"I do, but you don't."

"What?" I opened my calendar and a new meeting had literally just appeared. "Where did that come from? What's it about?"

"Client's worried about the change of head, wants to meet you, and I guess suss you out."

"Grmpf."

Sybil gave me a sympathetic look. "I know, but it shouldn't take long."

"I better go, looks like I'm already late." I grabbed cappuccino and notebook and was about to leave when I looked at my second drink. "Hey Sybil, do you want an extra hot cappuccino, no sugar? I've got one there, untouched. Help yourself."

Time to face the inquisition.

21

I used to think my days were mostly back-to-back meetings, with little time to do actual work in between, but those were nothing compared to my first day in Lynn's shoes.

I'd gotten crucified at the meeting with the client. Or roasted on hell's coal. They'd taken one look at me, and my fancy new haircut, and they'd decided I couldn't do the job, I was too young, too green, and they'd rather have someone more senior. They didn't say it, but I could see it in their eyes, hear it in their tone, what they really wanted was a man.

I understood that their company, which had just celebrated its hundred and fiftieth anniversary, was traditional, not to say conservative, but this was the twenty-first century for crying out loud. Why couldn't these male chauvinist dinosaurs accept that a woman could do the job just as well as a man, if not better? Jeff had backed me up, which I was grateful for, but it hadn't made the experience any less unpleasant. After that, I'd gone from useless meeting to useless meeting, facing consultants who were either completely unprepared, or who seemed to have called a meeting just for the pleasure of hearing themselves talk, or who'd brought problems, but no hint of solution.

I sat down at my desk, glad the last meeting of the day was over, and I would finally have a chance to get some work done when by phone vibrated. I unlocked the screen and saw the appointment reminder. *Shruti @ Police Station*. Bugger. I checked the time. I needed to leave right now if I was going to make it. I unplugged my laptop, not bothering to turn it off, and slipped it in my messenger bag along with my notebook. Tonight's evening entertainment would be sending out meeting minutes and action points and catching up on emails from the sofa. I didn't like this new trend, but Jasper would be thrilled.

Coat and scarf in hand, I ran out, almost knocking Millie over in the stairs.

"Sorry, can't talk, late," I called out. I should have taken the time to check she was all right, but she probably was, and I didn't have time to get sucked in chit chat and drama. I looked around the car park, trying to remember where I'd parked when it hit me. I'd walked in. My car was at home. Mental facepalm. I exited on foot and rang Shruti.

"Hi, it's Abigail, I'm going to be late, sorry, I'm on foot and got caught up in a meeting." I knew you were not supposed to lie to the police, but this was a white lie, and I wouldn't have been able to get out any earlier than I did even if I'd remembered I was car-less.

"No problem, how soon can you get here?"

"I'm guessing in about half an hour," I said, walking so fast I was already out of breath.

"No worries. I'll probably be here until about six anyway. Give me a call if there's a problem, I'll leave word at the front counter."

"Thanks, see you in a bit."

I dug out my earphones and launched my podcast app. I had a deeply curated playlist, that alternated life improvement with professional development podcasts, as well as one in French as I tried to retain the language skills that had taken me so long to acquire. I hit play, wondering what would come up, and it was one on life improvement. The speaker seemed to be madly in love with her houseplants, and thought anyone who didn't have a jungle at home was a loser who would die of multiple cancers because their air was not purified. I rolled my eyes, wishing I could stop walking for a couple of minutes to find something else. That person obviously didn't have a cat who would consider any patch of dirt an extension of his litter box, and any bit of green, including the *plastic* Christmas tree, as something to chew on to purge himself. She was also obviously home frequently enough to care for those plants. How was someone away four days a week every week supposed to water said plants?

I kept walking, trying to ignore the stitch forming in my right side. The road was busy this time of day, people coming home from work, or fetching children from after-school clubs, or doing a last-minute grocery run, and the petrol and diesel fumes stank up the air. At the first opportunity, I took a minute detour to land on a quieter side street that would lead me through the park before re-joining the main road and to the police station.

Lynn's husband Elliott was sitting on a bench in the park, talking on his phone. I couldn't hear the words, but as he saw me approaching, he fell silent. I waved at him, not breaking stride. He didn't look happy. Maybe he was on the phone with Lynn, trying to patch things up. I still didn't buy his story of her going to her mother's to take care of her, but the alternative was too bone-chilling to consider.

I pushed the door to the police station feeling hot and out of breath. Cardio exercise done for the day, ticked. Scratch that, that had to count for the whole week. I paused in the entrance area, gasping for air like a fish out of water. Water. I rummaged around my bag and dug out my bottle. I tipped it in my mouth but only a few drops came out. I'd been in such a hurry to leave I'd forgotten to refill it before leaving the office. The front counter area felt very warm, and I peeled off my coat, scarf, and cardigan. I felt sweaty. I put my hand to my forehead and got confirmation, I was literally dripping sweat. Lovely. I patted a tissue against my skin and walked to the front counter officer.

"Hi, I've got an appointment with Shruti Anand."

"Name?"

"Abigail Palmer."

The constable checked her clipboard and passed a piece of paper across the counter. "Print your name, address, number, time of entry, and who you're meeting on there, and take a seat, someone will come round to escort you," she instructed.

Not the friendliest, but I guessed that wasn't part of the job description. I complied, returned the sign-in sheet, and sat on the least dirty green-pleather bench lining the wall, grateful I hadn't worn my white trousers. I pulled out my work phone. If I had to wait, I might as well start catching up on emails. After the first five, I looked up from the tiny screen and blinked. Why would these people copy me in on stuff that had nothing to do with me? I didn't even need to be *aware* of any of it.

I tried to remember instances I'd copied project managers on emails. They were usually because there was a specific action for them to do, which I explicitly called out. Whether it was because it was their job, such as needing to progress a change request to the next stage, or because I needed them to tell the client to get on with it—although I usually did that myself—or because I needed them to impress on a team member the need to actually do their job, there was always something actionable.

In the five emails I'd just read, there was nothing, absolutely nothing for me to do, except maybe reply, 'why am I copied on this?' I returned my attention to the small screen. Boring, useless, and more boring.

"Abigail?" I looked up at Shruti. What must have started as a smart skirt suit this morning was definitely on the rumpled side of things now. "Sorry to keep you waiting."

"No problem, it's my fault I was late."

"Let's go this way."

I followed her through the double doors marked, 'restricted access, authorised personnel only,' along a magnolia-painted hallway, and into a small room. The police station was the old schoolhouse, and the room we were in looked like it had been a classroom at some point, but divided in three or four rooms to make offices and what appeared to be an interrogation room.

"Sorry about the interview room," Shruti said, "all the others are occupied at the moment."

My bad, I was about to be interviewed, not interrogated. I guessed journalists were closer to police officers than I thought.

"Take a seat, please. Do you want a drink? Tea, water? Coffee?"

"Water would be great actually."

I put my coat on the back of the uncomfortable-looking plastic chair and set my bag against one of the legs. I had to resist the urge to get my notebook out, so conditioned I was to set foot in a meeting room and start taking notes. This interview room was definitely meeting room-adjacent, with the uninspiring beige walls that were probably magnolia at some point in time, but lost their lustre over the years. The table was utilitarian, and appeared to be bolted to the floor. Four plastic chairs. A cable poking out from the middle of the table, presumably to plug in some kind of recording device. A coffee stain splashed on one of the walls was the only decoration. It looked like the police of Winburyton was seriously underfunded.

* * *

Shruti set the water in front of me and wrapped her hands around her tea for a second before getting a microphone out of her back pocket and plugging it in.

"That's just so we have a record and I don't have to ask you again what you said," she said as she plugged it into the cable poking out of the table.

Someone knocked on the door and Shruti called out to come in. A burly guy in a cheap suit walked in and took the chair next to Shruti.

Shruti spoke into the recorder. "This is Detective Sergeant Shruti Anand and Detective Constable Evan Robins interviewing Abigail Palmer."

She looked at me. "Abigail, DC Robins is going to listen in and take notes where pertinent. I will be leading this interview. You are here as a witness and are free to leave at any time or to request assistance from a solicitor should you want to, do you understand?"

I nodded. The whole thing sounded a lot more official and serious than I'd anticipated.

"We are here to discuss Lynn James, as I believe you have valuable information pertaining to her disappearance."

"She's disappeared?" Sounded like my initial instinct had been right.

"It appears so."

"Did her husband report her missing?"

"Sorry Abigail, I'm afraid I'm not authorised to answer your questions." Translation. Elliott had not reported her missing, and was therefore a suspect.

"Of course, sorry. Go ahead."

"When's the last time you saw Lynn?"

"Wednesday evening, when I left the office. She was still working."

"What was her mood that day? Did anything odd happen? Did she behave unusually?"

I thought back to the day, and also wondered whether to tell her about the note. Maybe if I did tell her about the note, it would help them find Lynn, but at the same time Lynn had been adamant I shouldn't tell the police about it.

A few seconds later I'd made up my mind. I'd answer her exact questions, and not the questions she wasn't asking.

"She was acting normal, barking at people, going from meeting to meeting. Normal stuff."

"So, nothing special, as far as you're aware, happened that day?"

I thought back. "Actually, there was one thing. I wouldn't call it special, but it's also not something that happens every day. A consultant was behaving like an ass, and it came out the next day that he got fired as a result."

Shruti leaned forward. "He acted like an ass to Lynn?"

DC Robins interjected. "What was his name?"

"Peter Dixon. And to answer Detective Sergeant Anand's question, he was an ass to a girl in the meeting I was in. I reported him to Lynn. She didn't want to do anything about it at first, but eventually I convinced her, and she said she was going to have a chat with him. The next day I heard he'd been fired, and Lynn hadn't shown up for work."

"Did that not surprise you?"

"Of course. I haven't worked with her for very long, but she didn't strike me as the kind of person who'd take a day off. She's too much of a control freak for that."

"You don't sound like you like her very much."

I shifted in the uncomfortable plastic chair. "No one does, as far as I can tell. Although I suppose her husband does, otherwise they wouldn't still be married."

"We were talking about you."

I thought about it while I sipped my water. "I don't like or dislike her. She's someone I'm currently working with, who seems to be competent at what she does. Beyond that, I can't say I agree with her methods or how she treats people, but I am terrible at dealing with people, so I'm not one to judge."

"I see. You mentioned her husband, do you know him well?"

"I don't. I must have seen him around obviously, since we both live Winburyton, but I didn't recognise him when I went to his office last week."

"Why did you go to his office?"

"I couldn't get hold of Lynn, her phone was going straight to voicemail, so I went to ask him how to get in touch with her."

Shruti frowned. "We'll come back to that. Yesterday, at the hairdressers, I heard you mention you got a promotion, correct?"

I couldn't wait to tell Hannah she'd been right, and Shruti had been eavesdropping. "I guess you can see it that way."

"Tell me about your promotion."

"More like a punishment really. I'm supposed to be doing my job *and* Lynn's job until she comes back."

"Isn't Lynn a lot more senior than you? I'm not judging, I'm assuming. She's quite a bit older than you, so it would make sense."

"Yes, you're right, she is."

"So that sounds like a major promotion?"

"More like a major pain in the ass."

"Didn't you want her job?"

I cocked my head to the side. I hadn't thought about this part. I'd thought at length about whether or not I could do both roles, and the consequences if I declined, but not about Shruti's question. Did I want to be project manager? It was something a lot of functional consultants I knew seemed to aspire to, in order to then ascend to programme director level, but was it what *I* wanted? Did I want the people management hassle and endless meetings?

"I didn't," I said.

"And now that you have the job?"

"I still don't want it. I maybe want it even less than I did before. And I've only done it for a day, so that says something."

I heard Shruti mutter under her breath that sounded like, 'the lady doth protest too much,' and I shifted in my chair before leaning forward.

"Listen, this job is just not me. I like my old job, and that's got scope for growth too. I like being hands-on, doing the practical stuff. It's varied too. This PM job is boring, it's basically pure admin."

"I see. Let's go back to Lynn's husband for a minute. What did you think when you met him?"

"Err . . ." I could tell her I had been wondering about buying chocolate direct from the factory next door, but something told me that wasn't what she wanted to hear. "Can you be more specific please?"

"Just in general. Did he seem happy? Excited? Depressed?"

I closed my eyes, trying to replay my meeting with Elliott as if it was a movie being projected on my eyelids. "Hassled."

"Huh?"

"Elliott seemed hassled. It could have been because of me though, I seem to have that effect on people."

"Interesting. What did you talk about?"

"Mostly the fact I couldn't reach Lynn."

"And what did he say about that?"

"That her mother was in hospital and that Lynn had gone up to take care of her."

"And what did he say about you not being able to reach her?"

"That she'd left her phone charger at home."

Shruti suddenly looked animated. "Did he say 'at home' exactly?"

"I don't know. Does it matter?"

"It might."

I thought back. Maybe Elliott had said at the house? Or . . . "I think his exact words were that she'd left it 'behind'."

"Interesting," Shruti repeated. "I think that's all I have for today."

Shruti rose from the chair and escorted me back to the front counter area. "Thank you for coming in, Abigail, can you make sure to keep yourself available if we have further questions?"

"As available as I can be doing two jobs," I said.

22

I got home and flopped on the sofa. My meeting with Shruti had left me mentally drained. Or maybe that interview had just been the cherry on an already exhausting day.

Jasper headbutted me. "Mrew."

I tried to scratch the bony little bump at the top of his head that made him purr like a freight train, but he walked away, just out of arm's reach. "What's up pussy cat? Don't you want pets?"

"Mrew," Jasper replied before disappearing to the kitchen. Moments later, he returned, tail flicking. "Mrew." He sat down at the kitchen door, tail flicking swiftly, sweeping the floor furiously.

I propped myself up on my elbow. "What do you want? I don't have the energy to play with you, sorry pussy."

"Mrew." Jasper went back to the kitchen where he continued issuing his short sharp meows.

Intrigued, I heaved myself out of the sofa and went to check on him. "What do you want?"

Jasper made figures of eight between my legs and carried on meowing.

"You're going to make me fall if you continue." He seemed to be guiding me to—"Oh, Jasper, I'm so sorry." I pulled the packet of dry food out of the cupboard and picked up the empty bowl from the floor. "I must have been distracted this morning," I said.

Maybe I was turning into a spinster, talking to my cat. Scratch that, I wasn't talking to my cat, I was having a *conversation* with him. I returned the full bowl to the floor, stroked Jasper's back as he dove into the bowl, and returned to the living room. The sofa looked so inviting, but I had work to do. I picked up the laptop and decided to settle at the dining table. It felt safer, somehow. At least the odds of me falling asleep in the chair were much lower than on the sofa. I could almost picture it, waking up in the morning, half of the keyboard imprinted on my cheek, maybe some drool on the trackpad. I shuddered. Nope, dining table was much safer.

At midnight, two hours past my bedtime, eyes closing on their own, I shut the laptop. So much wasted time. None but ten of those gazillion emails truly needed my input. And of those ten that did need my input, eight were sent to 'functional consultant' me, not 'project manager' me. Which meant that, in one day, my project manager self had received two hundred and twelve emails for no reason. I yawned as I dragged myself out to the bathroom. I would need to say something tomorrow at Sunrise, or this 'promotion' (I was now putting air quotes every time I thought of the word) would be the death of me before the end of the week.

I was putting on my pyjamas when I thought about my work phone. Had I turned on the do-not-disturb block? Last thing I needed was for it to start pinging at 4:30 a.m. when the Indian teams would be starting work.

I had a text from Millie.

Odd.

Odd that she would send a text instead of an instant message, and odd that she would text at all.

Curiosity took over being reasonable and I opened it. She'd sent it a few minutes before 10:00 p.m., and very sweetly told me to look after myself and that it was time to turn off the laptop and go to bed. Something about the message made me feel warm inside, a feeling I couldn't quite identify was spreading through my chest.

I'd thank her in the morning, didn't want to risk waking her by replying now. I set the DND and went to bed, giving Jasper, who was fast asleep at the foot of the bed, a death stare. I envied his ability to groom himself for five minutes, flop on the bed—or anywhere really—and then be fast asleep a minute later. Even if I did my yoga breathing exercises, I could almost guarantee it would take me at least an hour to fall asleep.

23

There was drumming going on in my head. Or in my dream. I couldn't hear the people around me anymore because the drumming was so loud. I couldn't breathe anymore, I felt oppressed by the atmosphere. A tiny bird flew past and pecked at my nose. I swatted it away and the bird had fur.

Apparently, this concept was too unbelievable for my brain and I woke up. Jasper was sitting on my chest, staring back at me, claws at the ready to take another pass at my nose.

"What the . . .?" I sat up, causing Jasper to roll down to the side. "Why d'you do that?" I felt for my nose. Blood. It was still dark outside, but I dragged myself out of bed anyway. Blood was a nightmare to get off sheets. I wagged my finger at the cat. "Bad Jasper." Not that he cared.

I was on my way to the bathroom when the drumming resumed. Except it wasn't drumming, it was pounding. Someone was pounding at my door, and my heart echoed it in anxiety.

I padded to the door, trying to be as quiet as possible so whoever was pounding wouldn't know I was here. I carefully slid the peephole cover to the side and peeked through at the pounder.

I pushed the cover back and let out a big sigh of relief as I unlocked the door.

"What the hell, Hannah? What time is it?"

Hannah put a bag of jam doughnuts in my hands and headed to the kitchen. "It's a few minutes before seven."

"Where are you going? What are you doing here at just before seven in the morning?"

"I'm going to make coffee, then I'll explain," Hannah called out from the relative depth of my small kitchen.

"I don't drink coffee first thing in the morning."

Hannah poked her head through the door. "You do today, trust me. Go brush your teeth or something, coffee will be ready in five minutes."

When Hannah was on a mission, there was little point fighting her. And she'd brought doughnuts. I went to the bathroom to tend to my nose, brushed my teeth while on the toilet, and got dressed before meeting Hannah back in the living room. She'd set the doughnuts on a plate, the coffee was ready as promised, with milk, honey, sugar, and cinnamon on the table, and, towering over the spread, her antique laptop presided.

"Why d'you bring your laptop?"

"Coffee first," Hannah ordered. "What happened to your nose?"

My hand flew to the clear plaster I'd put on my nose since the bleeding hadn't been kind enough to stop on its own. "Jasper. I guess your pounding annoyed him, so he took his claws to my nose to wake me up."

"Good boy," she said to Jasper who'd come looking for pets. He knew her well, since it was almost always Hannah who fed him when I was away.

I took a sip of coffee after adding a teaspoon of cinnamon and some honey and milk. "You didn't have to bang on the door so loud," I said grumpily. "If you'd waited until seven, I'd have been awake."

"Your alarm normally goes on at 5:30 a.m., which is not even a time normal people acknowledge exists, so frankly I expected to find you awake, yoga'd and dressed."

I grunted. "Late night. Changed my alarm to seven to catch up on sleep."

Hannah booted up the laptop. "Well, this couldn't wait. And I couldn't just text you either, who knew when you'd see it?"

"If this is about Angelina Jolie's new haircut, yes I have a thing for her, but it totally could have waited."

"It's not about your future wife. It's about the woman in the pond. Or Lady of the Lake as the journalists are calling her."

I sat up straighter and took a bite out of a jam doughnut. Hannah had been right, this definitely needed coffee. Sugar crystals fell on the table. Still holding the doughnut, and hoping no jam would ooze out, I pushed my chair back as Hannah's laptop started coming to life.

"Where are you going?" she asked.

"To the kitchen. We need plates and napkins, or this is going to get really messy."

"Well, hurry up."

"It's fine," I said with a smile, "I bet you I'll be back before your browser is even opened."

And I won my bet.

"What were you doing up so early anyway?" I asked, trying not to splutter bits of jammy doughnuts everywhere. "I thought you started at nine at the salon?"

"I do, but I had setup alerts everywhere I could think of on a bunch of keywords, so when the Winburyton chronicles updated their website two hours ago, my phone started beeping like mad."

"Smart about the alerts, but maybe you should have set up quiet hours on your phone?"

Hannah navigated to the Winburyton chronicle website and waited for the page to load. "Trust me, you'll be glad I didn't." Even though she was on my superfast Wi-Fi, her laptop was taking forever. Just like every time I saw it, I had an itch to run all sorts of cleaning, decluttering, and repair programs to speed it up. I was also willing to bet it had picked up a couple of viruses along the way, which would do nothing to help with the speed, not to mention potential theft of sensitive data.

The page finally loaded and my jaw dropped. Holy shit.

Town councillor named as Lady of the Lake.

I looked at Hannah. "You were right."

She nodded and scrolled down to the article. It didn't say much, just that the woman had been named as Lynn James, forty-eight, councillor of Winburyton, and that the police was exploring all avenues since it was treated as a suspicious death, and for any witnesses to, please, come forward.

"Either the police don't have much, or they didn't share with the journalists," I said.

"Don't you think it's strange they're just saying, 'suspicious death,' as if they think it could be something else than murder?" Hannah asked.

"Maybe. I suppose they have to consider other options, but maybe they want the killer to relax, thinking they've succeeded in fooling the police?"

"Or what if it was really an accident? Or a suicide?"

"Pretty sure it's not a suicide." I didn't know Lynn that well, but I couldn't see her killing herself, and definitely not by drowning herself in a pond. She was no Virginia Woolf. "I guess you can consider an accident, but then, what was she doing by the pond? She'd probably have gone there fairly late at night, or someone would have seen her."

"Does it have to be late at night?" Hannah asked, eating her second doughnut.

"She left me a voicemail at 10:35 p.m., so it had to be after that. And there are a few pubs in the area, so if it had been before last call, people might have seen her. After eleven however, I doubt there would have been anyone around." I thought about it for a beat. "It really must have been important, it's been cold at night."

Hannah nodded. "I know, I got my winter duvet out weeks ago." She took another doughnut from the plate. "Now what?"

"Now I go to work, tell my big boss the news, beg for him to find a replacement asap, and try to clear my name so I don't end up in prison, I suppose?"

24

"You're joking," Jeff said. A statement, not a question.

I'd taken him to a meeting room as soon as I'd gotten in the office, and broke the news as gently as I could. I'm guessing not gently enough, because Jeff was floored. Maybe I'd been too abrupt. I'd been told so in performance reviews before. Needed to be more sensitive. Needed to be more aware of people's feelings.

Screw that, no way I was going to turn into a fluffy, touchy-feely person. I was who I was, I knew who I was, and while I was all for personal improvement, I was totally against attempting a personality transplant. Smoothing the edges, yes, removing them, no.

I sighed as I unlocked the laptop. "Jeff . . . Three things." I pushed the laptop aside. "When have you ever seen me joke?" I held my fist up with the thumb out as I listed them. "Do I look like I'm joking?" Got my index out. "What kind of sick bastard would be joking about something like that?" I'd scrunched up my face when I said that last one, because frankly, that would really be sick.

Jeff stared wordlessly at my thumb, index, and middle fingers before rubbing his hands on his face. "Shit."

"Yes." I pushed my laptop in front of him. "Here's the article, but it's not going to tell you much more than I did."

Jeff read through it. "They say the police thinks she died last week."

"Right."

"Why would her husband call me on Friday night to say she was at her mother's for an indeterminate period of time?"

I could think of only two possible answers. Either he genuinely believed she'd gone away, or he was responsible for her death and was trying to cover his ass. I didn't share those thoughts with Jeff though, just like I hadn't shared everything with Shruti. Maybe I should tell her about the note now. Lynn's privacy didn't really matter anymore, she was dead. But, what if Shruti thought it was suspicious that I hadn't told her about the note in the first place? What if she thought I was the murderer? She already thought I'd been after Lynn's job all along, what if she thought I'd made up the note as a way to send the investigation in another direction?

Jeff's question was still hanging in the air. "I don't know." I looked up at the wall clock. It was just after eight o'clock. "Jeff, you have to announce it to the team at Sunrise."

Jeff started in his chair. "Me?"

I cocked my head to the side. "Jeff, you're the most senior person on the project."

"But I haven't processed yet. *You* have. Why don't you do it? You're pretty senior now."

Unbelievable. How could he be trying to weasel out of this? And he seemed to be forgetting an important point. "That's something else I wanted to talk to you about. You have to find a permanent replacement for Lynn, and fast. I cannot do both roles at the same time."

"Come on Abigail, you don't think I have enough on my plate right now?"

Privately, I thought he didn't. He didn't because he'd pushed everything from his plate to mine, just like I did with any olives that landed on my pizza. I picked them out one by one, and pushed the lot onto someone else's plate. The difference was that I asked the person first, did they want my olives? Even Hannah, who always said yes. But Jeff hadn't asked me anything. He'd just dumped the lot in my lap.

I looked at him. He was scrolling up and down the article, over and over, as if trying to learn new information. As if *hoping* new information had magically appeared.

Maybe I would wait. He didn't look like he would be able to hear anything I had to say. Or any threats I wanted to make.

25

"Do you think I should call her husband?" Jeff's voice sounded broken, as if he was the one who'd been personally affected by Lynn's death. I tried to remember if he was married, but nothing came to mind. He didn't wear a ring, but that didn't mean anything. Some people didn't want to wear them.

"That's up to you." What the hell was I supposed to answer? "We should get going or we'll miss Sunrise."

"Maybe we should wait until the end to tell them." I gave Jeff a what-the-hell-are-you-on-about look. "If we tell them at the beginning, they'll shut down and won't hear the meeting."

I felt my eyes straining in their sockets, ready to jump out, turn into mini grenades, and explode on Jeff.

"Jeff," I said in a voice I tried to keep calm, even though I was shaking with rage inside. "How would *you* feel, if I went through a twenty-minutes meeting, and then, at the end of it, as part of the 'any other business' topics, alongside the fact that there was a fire alarm testing planned for later, and that there would be a biscuit delivery in the afternoon, I announced, 'oh, and by the way, your boss is dead, and the circumstances are suspicious'? Come on, be sensible," I pleaded.

Jeff opened his mouth to reply, but I shut him down. "And don't forget, while the majority of people on our side don't read the Winburyton chronicles, the client people probably do. And even if they don't, it would have popped up on their social media feeds, I guarantee it, which means our side knows too now. You have to get in front of this."

Jeff held his hands up. "Okay, okay, enough, I'm with you. We get to the meeting, you tell them, and then what?"

"Then we ask if there are any questions, and if there aren't any, we apologise for moving on to the project stuff but we do move on. If there are questions, you need to accept that there probably won't be much work done today."

"Christ. Okay, fine. Let's get in there."

His sudden mellowing in the face of a full day delay seemed suspicious, just like his enthusiasm to get into the meeting to announce the death of his direct report, but that probably had more to do with the fact he didn't have to make the announcement. I did.

26

As I'd anticipated, my announcement of Lynn's death was met with stunned silence. Even if no one liked Lynn, it would have been quite a leap for anyone to wish her death. Her death for real that is. Because, honestly, I didn't know anyone who'd never wished to kill a project manager at some point.

There had been a few questions, but thankfully those were around chain of command and project work, rather than about the events surrounding her death. All I would have been able to say on the latter was what had been in the two newspaper articles, and that wasn't much. Jeff took the questions around chain of command, identifying me as Lynn's replacement. A senior consultant asked if it was realistic to expect me to do both roles, and I looked pointedly at Jeff. 'I told you so,' I said telepathically. It wasn't just me, it wasn't about having impostor syndrome. It really was about the fact that it was too much for one person.

"I have only just now been made aware of the news myself," Jeff said, looking appropriately sombre, "so I have not had a chance to discuss the matter with our resourcing department, however I will be having a call with them later this morning, and I expect I will receive profiles of suitable candidates over the next couple of days."

Cue sigh of relief on my part. Assuming Jeff meant what he'd just said. I wouldn't put it past him to say one thing and do another. He was a politician. That was another reason I didn't want the job. I didn't have an ounce of diplomacy, or any ability to navigate office politics. I wanted to go in, do my job, go home. Not jump through hoops like a circus tiger. Or a dolphin in an aquatic park.

The consultants nodded, visibly feeling the same relief I did.

"Any other question on the topic?" I asked. I waited a few seconds, but no one said anything. "I know this has been a shock for everybody, but unfortunately we still have a project to deliver. And anyone who knew Lynn, even if only a little, knows that if she'd had someone sadly pass away on one of her projects, she would have run the project as usual." A few consultants nodded in the crowd, and, out of the corner of my eye, I caught Jeff nodding as well. "Let's start with Finance. Ram, you're replacing Peter, right? Any updates, blockers, areas of concerns?"

The rest of meeting went more or less as usual, maybe a little subdued, but, overall, no one seemed too fazed by Lynn's demise.

Given the circumstances, I decided to not do the speech I'd planned about unnecessary emails. Instead, I went back to my desk and crafted an out-of-office email that would be sent to anyone emailing me.

> Thank you for your email. Please note that I am currently receiving an extremely high volume of email, most of them irrelevant. All emails sent after 10pm last night have been deleted. If you have an action for me, please come talk to me directly.

I called Sybil over. "Can you have a look at this and let me know if this is fine please?"

Sybil was reading over my shoulder when Millie walked up to me. "Are you all right?" she asked. "Is there anything I can do?"

"Actually, can you read over this auto-reply as well, please? I asked Sybil to take a look, but two pairs of eyes from people much more diplomatic than me can't hurt."

She leaned over my other shoulder and started reading. Sybil was done, and was waiting quietly for Millie to be done too.

"So? What do you think?" I asked when they were both done.

"I think it's fine," Sybil said.

"No, you need to remove the bit about the emails being irrelevant," Millie said.

"But they are," I protested. "Seriously, yesterday, I had over two hundred, and only ten were relevant."

Millie straightened up. "I get it, but trust me. Change management is my job, and that's basically what you're trying to do. You're implementing a change to the process. Don't tell people they're stupid if you want them to follow the new process."

"Okay, fine." I deleted the offending sentence. "Anything else?"

"What if all the people who emailed you yesterday descend on your desk because they all think it's important and you need to do something?"

Sybil raised her hand and we turned to her. "Maybe I could filter the emails? I've been dying to take on more responsibilities, but Lynn never let me do anything except accept meeting invites on her behalf, and then she'd still insist on reviewing everything."

I stared at her, but I wasn't looking at her anymore. I was in my head, running the scenarios to see if her proposal could work.

"I mean, obviously I couldn't vet the questions on the Sales side, but I really think I can help on the project management side of things, I just need you to give me a chance," she pleaded.

I looked at Millie, trying to read her mind, trying to figure out if she thought it was a good idea or a disaster waiting to happen.

"I think it's a great idea," she said, as if she'd known what I was wondering.

"Okay. Let's give it a try. Let's call it, 'Testing Cycle One.' We'll catch up last thing tonight, see how it went, and we'll tweak the process if necessary, okay?"

Sybil nodded, and her eyes were misting up.

"Sybil, I swear, if you cry, I'm taking it back. I can't deal with tears."

Sybil fled out of the office.

"Argh." I looked at Millie. "How do you do it?"

"What?"

"Deal with people's emotions on a daily basis. You must have seen your fair share of tears and tantrums in your role. Why would you even *want* to be in change management?"

Millie smiled. "For you, human emotions are hell. For me, they're heaven."

I winced.

"No, seriously. I've got a master's in psychology, and this role is almost exactly what I wanted to do. One day I'll tell you why I wanted to do this, maybe over a couple of drinks, but you've got more important things to deal with right now. I think you should tweak the autoreply a bit to reflect that Sybil will be filtering your PM requests. I also think you should send it as a regular email now, a pre-emptive strike of sorts."

That made sense. I set to redraft the message. "How's that?"

> Thank you for your email. Please note that I am currently receiving an extremely high volume of emails. If you have an action for me as project manager, please contact Sybil Johnson in the first place.
>
> If your action or question relates to the Sales workstream, please ensure to have "Sales Workstream" in the subject of your email. Anyone found to abuse the "Sales Workstream" tag will be blocked.

Millie smiled. "Almost perfect. I would add something at the end thanking them for their understanding during the transition."

I must have pouted, because Millie laughed. "Come on, it doesn't hurt to be polite."

"Fine." Was I too old to stamp my feet? "I should probably run this by Jeff, just in case some people take offence. Thank you for your help," I added as an afterthought.

Millie beamed at me. "Anytime."

* * *

Laptop under my arm, I went over to Jeff's desk. He was staring in space, apparently deep in thoughts since he didn't react to my, 'Hey Jeff, do you have a minute?' I gingerly poked him in the shoulder. Last thing we needed was for him to have a stroke or something. He jumped when my finger dug into the soft flesh. "Careful Abigail, you don't go around prodding people like that. You need to ask for permission before touching anyone."

"I tried talking to you first," I defended myself, "but you seemed miles away."

His face relaxed into a pained smile. "Yeah. Did you notice no one seemed sad at Sunrise? None of them seemed to even care she was dead. What's wrong with these people?"

"You can't hold it against them. She was basically a stranger for ninety percent of them, and for the remaining ten percent who had regular interactions with her, she made their life hell. What did you expect?"

Jeff sighed. "I don't know. Not this. She was such a strong woman, with her own opinions, she went after what she wanted, but she wasn't all serious all the time, she could be fun too."

Lynn? Fun? If I were a cartoon character, I'd be having a ton of question marks popping above my head right now. "How so?"

A smile hovered on his lips. "There was this time, we had dinner and midway through the first course she—" Jeff stopped himself, as if suddenly aware of my presence. His smile faded, he straightened in his chair. "I'm sorry, I'm digressing. Did you want something?"

"Yes. Like I said this morning, the workload isn't manageable, so I want to set an out of office reply asking people to stop sending me irrelevant stuff."

His eyebrows knitted together. "I don't think this is very appropriate—"

"Jeff, I'm not asking for your permission. I'm telling you what I'm doing, so that if there are repercussions, you know what it's about."

"I think power is already going to your head, but let's

see it." He read the email under his breath. "I'm really not happy with you sending this email Abigail."

"And I'm really not happy with you sticking me this second full-time job on top of the first one without much support."

"Grmpf."

"Unless you have anything you want me to tweak in the wording, this is going out to everybody in the next minute."

"Careful Abigail, I'm still the programme director here."

"Then act like one. I'm assuming you already notified HR and whoever is the head of her team at HQ. How about the Indian teams? Did you notify them yet?" I didn't wait for his answer and stomped back to my desk. A part of me was anxious, thinking I'd not only crossed a line, but danced in front of the tiger, and there would be painful payback coming my way. The optimistic side of me was thinking I'd asserted myself and Jeff would respect me more for it. The combination of the two made me a nervous wreck.

Sybil was back at her desk. "Everything okay?"

"I don't know." There was something in Jeff's attitude to Lynn's death that bothered me. He seemed abnormally grief-stricken. I leaned back in my chair and nervously tapped my pen against my hand. I was missing something that was right in front of me, and it bothered me. I replayed our conversations, from early this morning and from a few minutes ago, pausing on every detail, his posture, his tone of voice, his facial expressions.

"Do you know if Jeff had worked with Lynn before?" I asked Sybil.

"Didn't you know? They've been a sort of package deal forever. From what I heard, at the beginning, they just happened to land on the same projects, but when Jeff started being able to choose his own team, he always brought Lynn on."

"And nobody commented on it?"

Sybil shrugged.

Of course. There would have been gossip at the beginning, then people would have lost interest, and it would have become the accepted thing.

How could I have been so blind? He and Lynn weren't just colleagues, or even just friends. They had been having an affair.

27

I got another visit from Shruti. This time, she was accompanied by DC Robins, and they were standing right by my desk.

"Miss Palmer, could you join us at the police station please?" DC Robins said.

My stomach rumbled. It was past 5:00 p.m., it had been another manic day, I hadn't had anything except for the 7:00 a.m. doughnuts and a couple of biscuits as a makeshift lunch and I was now desperate for some real food. Preferably comfort food. Maybe mac and cheese. Or chilli con carne. Something like that. "Now?"

"We appreciate this is short notice," Shruti said, "but we would really appreciate your cooperation."

"What about my car?"

"You can drive down," Shruti said, "I'll come with you."

Uh-oh. It sounded like I was in big trouble. They wouldn't have come to get me in person, and Shruti wouldn't be riding in my car, if I wasn't a serious suspect. What had happened for them to upgrade me from witness to suspect?

We drove down in silence, Shruti probably trying to make me sweat, me simply being peopled out and not wanting to engage in strenuous small talk. When we walked through the doors of the police station, Shruti took me by the elbow and guided me to an interrogation room in the newer wing.

"What's going on Shruti?"

"It's DS Anand in here, Miss Palmer." That was me told. "But I will tell you what's going on. New evidence has come to light. We were given permission to examine Mrs James's phone records, both personal and professional . . ."

Shit.

"We found that Mrs James had called you the night she disappeared, and you talked for twenty-eight seconds. What was it about?"

"We didn't talk."

DC Robins shifted his bulky figure in the chair. "Miss Palmer. The phone records clearly show that Mrs James' professional phone called your professional number, and that this call lasted for twenty-eight seconds. There is no point in you denying this, we have evidence."

"We didn't talk," I insisted. "I was home, I'd already put my phone on 'do not disturb' for the night. I didn't notice Lynn had called me until the next morning."

"You often put your phone on silent? What if there had been a problem at work?"

I mentally rolled out my eyes. "I deal with computer systems for a *biscuit* factory. That's hardly life and death, not as if I was a doctor or a police officer. And we aren't in a cutover period, when we would need to be working around the clock to ensure the systems go-live correctly."

Shruti made a note on her clipboard. "I see. In that case, the only explanation for the length of that call is that she left you a voicemail . . .."

I stayed silent. If they asked me to play Lynn's voicemail, then I'd have to explain about the threat notes.

DC Robins carried on. "Or that you're lying to us, that

you did pick up the phone, and that you went to meet Lynn somewhere."

"I didn't pick up," I repeated.

"Then she left you a voicemail," Shruti said. "What was it about?"

"She wanted to remind me that I needed to have the next round of updates to my workstream's process design documents done by the morning. I'd forgotten to do it that morning, and she'd had to remind me. Lynn's a control freak. She always reminds . . . reminded people to do things several times, even if they have the task in hand. Control freak."

"That sounds a lot like resentment," Shruti observed.

"More like a fact. It's not the end of the world though, I would only have had to deal with her until the end of the project. Then we'd both move on to other projects, and probably never work together again."

"And when is that?" Shruti asked. "The end of the project."

I sighed. "In theory, according to the plan that's already been reworked three times—and each time Lynn and Jeff said it was the last time—another eight months."

"You don't sound convinced?"

My vision blurred, the same way it always did when I was thinking deeply about something. "We'll see," I eventually said. I'd realised I couldn't share my thoughts with Shruti, the risk of it going back to someone on the client's side was too big. Because, of course, that latest project plan was still completely unrealistic. Based on what I'd seen in the last five weeks, and my decade of project experience, we'd be lucky if we went live in the next eighteen months. And I thought I was being generous here.

"You do know that, even if you deleted the voicemail, we can ask your mobile phone carrier to recover it?" DC Robins said.

I had to tell them the truth, or, at the very minimum, I'd end up being locked up for twenty-four hours. "Fine. Lynn didn't call me about design documents. She was being blackmailed, and she called me to tell me that she'd found a second note when she got home that night. I didn't listen to the voicemail until the next morning."

DC Robins leaned forward. "So, for the record, you're admitting to lying, and obstruction of the investigation."

"Lynn had told me very specifically to not mention the threat note to the police. She sort of blackmailed me into figuring out who had sent her the note. I told her to report it to the police, but she wouldn't hear of it."

Shruti cocked her head to the side. "Why did she ask you? Why did she blackmail you? What made you qualified to investigate a threat?"

I wasn't sure what was happening. Maybe it was the pressure, but I'd always thrived under pressure. So that didn't explain why I suddenly felt very tearful. I took a sip of water from my bottle. "You're right, I'm not qualified. At all. There's no contest there. But Lynn had heard I was fascinated by Sherlock Holmes and his methods, and she decided it made me qualified," I muttered through gritted teeth.

"I'm sorry, can you repeat that last bit? What did Lynn hear about you?"

"That I'm a Holmesian."

Shruti's lips parted before she pulled herself together. "You're a what?"

"A Holmesian. Someone who admires Sherlock Holmes, and tries to apply his methods," I repeated.

"You do realise he's a fictional character?" DC Robins was looking at me as if I was deluded.

"Of course. But Arthur Conan Doyle based Sherlock Holmes on a real person, a doctor he'd worked with, Joseph Bell. The principle of deductive reasoning combined with careful observation is sound."

DC Robins leaned back in his chair and smiled a slightly evil smile. "Fine. Tell me something about me then."

* * *

I took a deep breath. I hated being put on the spot like that, and I wished people would just believe me. "Fine. But I'm not an expert. You injured your right ankle at least twenty years ago, it was a minor injury. You recently separated from your wife. You left her because you met someone new. You've recently taken up cooking, but you're not very good at it."

DC Robins stared at me as if his eyes were going to pop out of their orbits and a crimson tint was on his cheeks.

Shruti turned to him. "You and Laura split up? When? Why didn't you say anything?"

"It's private, I didn't need the whole police station to know my personal business. We split up two weeks ago."

Shruti glanced at me before returning to Evan. "And the rest? The ankle injury, the cooking?"

He replied through gritted teeth. "It's true. And I'm not that bad at cooking."

Shruti returned to me. "How did you know?"

"The separation is because of his ring finger. He keeps on rubbing it as if he is trying to turn a ring. He wouldn't still be doing it if he'd taken his ring off a long time ago. He

150

seems to have lost weight and gained muscles, judging by the way his shirt is slightly baggy at the stomach but taut at the torso, so I'm guessing he's been hitting the gym pretty hard, which suggests he met someone new a while ago. The cooking is obvious, he's got lots of tiny cuts on his fingers, which would have been done because of poor knife skills, suggesting a beginner cook. Typically food prepared by beginner cooks isn't that great."

"How'd you know about my ankle?" DC Robins asked.

"Your gait. It's very slight, but your left shoulder is a little bit higher than your right."

"How'd you connect his shoulders to an ankle injury?" Shruti looked mystified.

"The shoulders, hips, knees, ankles, it's all connected. If you have injured your ankle and don't have any physio after, you get into bad postural habits. DC Robins probably started walking on his ankle before it was healed, which led to knee pain because the lateral movement the ankle couldn't produce was transferred to the knee, but the knee joint isn't supposed to move laterally, so he subconsciously adjusted his posture to compensate."

I stopped to take a sip of water. Both police officers were looking at me as if I was from Mars. "I suggest you work on improving your ankle flexibility and strength, as well as strengthening all the muscles in your right leg, by working them in isolation. It will take a long time to correct the issue, but you'll eventually be pain-free. Oh, and it will fix your lower right butt cheek."

"WHAT?"

"I'm just saying. I'm only trying to help. And you're the one who wanted me to tell you about you."

Shruti, thankfully, backed me up. "She's right, Evan. You did ask."

DC Robins sunk back deeper in his plastic chair, and I wondered if he was going to slide off.

"Let's get back to Lynn," Shruti said. "She wanted you to investigate. Investigate what exactly?"

"She'd received a note in an envelope. No address, just an initial and last name. Someone had put it through her mailbox."

"Where is that note now?" DC Robins asked.

"I have it at home."

"What did the note say?" Shruti asked.

"Tell the truth or I will."

DC Robins looked suspicious. "That's it?

"No, there was also a drawing."

"What did the drawing represent?" Shruti seemed really animated, almost as if I was giving them a strong lead.

"It was six triangles arranged around a circle. May I?" I pointed at Shruti's pen and clipboard.

She pushed them both across the table and I drew the symbol. "That's what it looks like."

"Did Lynn show the note to her husband?"

"I don't know. I'm guessing not, she was really adamant I shouldn't talk about it with anyone."

"Did you find out who sent the note? Or what's that truth the note is talking about?"

I briefly debated telling them about Frank's tattoo, but it seemed unfair. What if he had nothing to do with it? He would get so much hassle, and it could seriously hurt his business. Besides, I couldn't see him hurting Lynn. He wasn't the type.

"No, I made no progress. The fact that Lynn refused to tell me anything about . . . well, about anything, rather impeded my investigation, if you want to call it that."

"We'll need this note," DC Robins said, "although I'm not sure how much help it will be. And we'll need your prints for elimination purposes."

"Sure. I handled the note and the envelope as little as possible, but yes, you'll find my prints on it. And my cat's."

DC Robins frowned. "Your cat's?"

"He stepped on the note once. It was an accident."

DC Robins looked up to the ceiling, and I could have sworn he'd muttered 'good god' under his breath.

"Tell us about Mrs James's voicemail," Shruti said.

"I can play it for you," I offered, pointing at my bag. "It's still on my work phone."

"Why did you keep it?" DC Robins asked.

"I didn't 'keep it,' I just didn't delete it. Don't you ever just listen to a voicemail and hang up, without waiting for the menu to come up, and then press button x, and then key y, and then wait for confirmation the message has been deleted? I'm pretty sure it will say I have at least ten 'saved' messages. I haven't actually 'saved' them, I just haven't actively deleted them."

"Alright, we got it Miss Palmer, play the message, please."

I pulled my work phone out and dialled the voicemail number on speakerphone. As expected, it said I had nineteen saved messages.

When the message was done playing, I hung up and looked at the two police officers across the table. "See? It doesn't tell you anything, except that she was annoyed I didn't pick up the phone."

My stomach rumbled loudly, echoing through the sparsely furnished room. "If this is going to go on for much longer, I'm going to need food," I announced. "An hour ago, I was merely hungry, now I'm starving." The clock on the wall showed it was after six o'clock. Not that late, unless you hadn't had anything all day, save for some biscuits.

Shruti stood and nodded at Evan, who heaved himself out of the chair. "Give us a minute Miss Palmer, we'll be back soon."

While they were gone, I wondered how much trouble I was in. Not a lot, I hoped, since I'd helped by telling them about the note. Better late than never, right?

28

When they walked back into the room, I'd been waiting for fifteen minutes. Was it what they called 'soon'? I needed to eat something, or I would faint as soon as I tried rising from my chair. I wondered if I still had a lollipop in my bag?

"We discussed your case with the SIO—" Shruti said.

"—SIO?"

DC Robins replied, "Senior Investigating Officer. The person in charge of the team investigating the death of Mrs James." He still looked sour. Maybe I'd pushed the detection too far, but he'd asked for it. He gave me a look, as if challenging me to say something, anything, but I remained quiet.

"Anyway, the SIO agreed to not keep you any longer. We will accompany you back to your flat to retrieve the note and envelope, and then we'll be out of your life," Shruti said.

DC Robins smirked. "That is, unless we find out other instances of you lying to us, in which case we will promptly charge you with everything we can, arrest you, and send you to prison for what will hopefully be a very long time."

I'd never had a nemesis or a mortal enemy before, especially not one who had power like he did. Was he a Moriarty or a Milverton though?

"When can we go? I'm famished."

"I almost forgot," Shruti said. She searched in her trousers' pocket and extracted a granola bar she pushed across the table. "Not the healthiest, since it's full of sugar, but it's probably exactly what you need."

I nodded and set to work on the packaging. It was one of those easy openings that never were easy. In a way, they were like Rubik's cube, if you knew how to solve the puzzle, it was really easy, but if you had to figure it out for yourself, it took ages.

I finally got the packaging to open and took a bite of the bar, letting it melt on my tongue rather than chewing up. In my mind, it made the sugar delivery faster. I'd need to check for future reference.

"Ready?" Shruti asked.

I followed them out to the car park.

"I'll ride with you," Shruti told me. "DC Robins will follow us in his car so he can drive me back."

"Or you could walk," I suggested. It wasn't that far, twenty minutes at most.

"Like you," she replied as she got in the passenger seat of my car, "I want to get home as soon as possible."

They came in my flat, picked up the note, and left without attempting to do any kind of searching, so I figured I was in the clear, for now. Once I'd locked the door after them, I called out for Jasper and set to search.

I found him on the first try. He was highly predictable, just like me. Neither one of us liked it, but there wasn't much either one of us could do to change it.

"Come on you big wuss, you can come out now, the other humans are gone and aren't coming back." Or at least I hoped they wouldn't. Jasper was rooted very firmly under the sofa, laying not quite flat enough that I'd be able to drag him out, and was showing no sign of moving.

I let him be, filled up his food bowl, and put my lunchbox in the sink. I did my best to carry on as normal, but the last few days had been anything but normal. I took whatever food was in the fridge that didn't need prepping and took it to the living room. The cheese would need to get to room temperature before it was edible, but that was fine. I had leftover bresaola and carrot sticks, and I could make an emergency cup noodle. It was just boiling water and pouring, it hardly counted as cooking.

I texted Hannah.

> Me: Everybody hates me at work. Got interrogated by the police for the second time. Having a no-cook dinner. How was your day?

She replied a few minutes later.

> Hannah: OMG what happened
>
> Hannah: Im on my way over

A part of me, okay, most of me . . . fine, ninety-nine percent of me screamed NOOOOOO. I didn't want to people anymore. Talking left me drained so badly my brain felt like mush. I loved Hannah to bits, but her enthusiasm often sapped whatever energy I had left. But then there was a tiny part of myself telling me that, actually, not being on my own tonight, and getting a big hug from a friend, could be just what I needed. I texted back.

> Me: OK, see you soon

I went to the bedroom to change out of my work clothes. They felt stiff and rigid, as if they would stifle all creative thinking, and I had a feeling Hannah and I were about to be very creative in our discussions.

29

Hannah sat cross-legged on my couch, a bottle of non-alcoholic cider in her hand. That's the thing I liked about Hannah. She knew I didn't entertain, so she brought her own drinks, of her own accord, saving me agonising over what kind of beverage to buy for guests.

"But that's ridiculous," she said, "why would you kill Lynn?"

"They thought I wanted her job."

"But you didn't—"

"Still don't."

"Right. And even if you did, how could you have known they would give it to you? Didn't you say it was a really senior role?"

"It is."

"Then shouldn't it have gone to someone more senior? As in, someone old?"

I smiled in spite of myself at Hannah's bluntness. "You're right my lovely, it should have."

"Then it was dumb luck or something, not careful planning."

I nodded. "One thing I want to figure out is who *did* kill her. Because someone did, and it wasn't me."

"How are you going to figure that out? You don't have the resources the police have, like access to CCTV, or DNA testing, or anything like that."

"You're right, although I doubt they recovered much physical evidence, not with her body being in the water. It probably destroyed everything."

"Then how are you going to figure it out?"

"I don't know. If we were in a Sherlock Holmes story, he would disguise himself and start nosing around. Or he would sit in his armchair and turn the facts until they fit, then he'd go out and get the evidence that confirms his theory."

"I'm guessing you're not going to play dress-up?"

"No, and I can't exactly sit at home for a week to figure it out either."

"Then what?"

I could only see one option. "We brainstorm."

"As in . . . you and I?" Hannah asked, sounding dubious.

"Sure, why not?" Without waiting for her answer, I started. "Statistically, homicides are committed by people the victim knows. It would make sense here too, because I can't see Lynn going for a midnight stroll alone in the park on her own on a weeknight. She had to have been meeting someone."

"What if she did go for a midnight stroll?"

"But it doesn't make sense based on what I knew about her."

"Hear me out," Hannah insisted. "What if she did go for a stroll, but she wasn't on her own."

I pondered Hannah's words. "A lover . . . there's someone at work I think she might have been having an affair with."

"Or her husband. Didn't you say he didn't seem happy about her being home every night? Maybe they were talking about separating?"

"Elliott? Why kill her, when he could just divorce her?"

"Why do spouses kill each other?"

"Love, jealousy, which I guess falls under love, anger, money . . . Wait a second . . . The money. If they divorced . . . but no . . ."

Hannah rolled her eyes. "Can you finish a sentence already?"

I rubbed my forehead. "Sorry, just trying to order my thoughts. We know he needed money, right, since he's been transferring money from the joint account into his company's account. But, if they divorced, he would have gotten half of their assets, but only half. If he killed her, he'd get to keep all the money. Unless there's a will that says Lynn's money is going to her mother. But murder is so messy. And I'm pretty sure even only half of their assets would still be more than enough for him to live on comfortably."

Hannah sat back on the sofa, sipping her cider, clearly mulling a thought over. "What about love?" she eventually asked. "Remember? Lynn told me she thought he was having an affair?"

"So, Elliott potentially has two strong motives to have killed Lynn . . . we just need to find some proof."

"How are you going to do that?" Hannah asked.

I chewed on my lower lip, wishing, not for the first time, that I had a pencil on hand instead. Chewing on something tangible helped me think (gum didn't do it for me), but using body parts was not the smartest thing. "I guess I have to find out if he has an alibi."

"How? Are you going to visit him at the office again, and just casually ask him where he was the night his wife was murdered?"

I opened my mouth, but nothing came out. I knew I couldn't do that, but I had no idea what I *could* do.

"If only I knew who he hangs out with. Maybe I could sort of ask them. You don't know by any chance?"

Hannah shook her head no.

"Are people talking about Lynn's death at the salon? A murder in Winburyton, that's got to be a hot topic, no?"

Hannah winced.

"What?"

"Today was my day off, I wasn't at the salon, sorry. I'm working tomorrow, I can keep an ear out?"

"Please do. I'll go to the shops after work tomorrow, maybe I can casually ask questions."

Hannah's face was painted with worry.

"What?"

She scouted over on the sofa until she was next to me. She wrapped an arm around my shoulders and squeezed tight. "Sweetie, you know I love you to bits, right?"

I nodded, taken aback.

"So I am going to say this with all my love. Subtle and casual are not your strong points."

I was offended. Pure and simple. How dared she say I couldn't be subtle. "That is so uncalled for. Of course I can do subtle."

I'd show her. I would get Elliott's alibi before she knew it, by any means necessary.

Hannah shuffled in her seat. "Hey, I've got an idea. Let's go to the pub."

I raised an eyebrow. "To the pub. On a weeknight? No thanks."

"Come on Abigail, it's barely eight o'clock."

"No way. Why would I want to subject myself to a bunch of drunkards on a school night?"

Hannah rose. "Just because once, seven years ago, one drunk guy grabbed your ass doesn't mean it's going to happen again. It's not even the same landlord anymore. We're down there almost every Friday nights, you know it's fine."

The rational part of my brain knew she was right. The Dark Horse was fine, hardly anyone bothered me when I went there, included on Saturday nights when they had live music. But that part of my brain also seemed to shrink back as the day went on, until any excuse would do if it meant I didn't have to *people* anymore.

"I've already changed," I said showing my comfy bottoms. "I took off my bra."

Hannah forced me out of the sofa. She'd shown deceptively high strength for such a small person. "Go put a bra on, and some going out clothes. We're going and that's final."

"Why do you even want to go?" I asked.

"Because the Lady of the Lake's identity was released today. If we go now, we have a chance to catch the people who've stopped by for a drink before going home. And those who came in for a post-dinner drink. Come on, it's perfect!"

My heart raced. It was human nature. The more horrific the crime, the more people wanted to talk about it. "Give me two minutes thirty seconds," I said before running out of the room.

30

The pub wasn't far, walking distance from both our places. I followed Hannah in, already feeling out of place. Eyes followed us as we walked around the U-shaped bar to get to the other side, where it was less crowded, and waited for the bar staff to notice us. Hannah whispered at me. "See? Told you the place would be packed. Now you just need to work the room."

Right. Work the room. How was one supposed to do that?

Hannah seemed to have read my mind. "Just relax. Walk around, make eye contact with people. You're always complaining that people you don't know come up to you and make small talk. Or try to, given that you shut them down at 'hello.' Use that to your advantage."

"But that's the problem. When people talk to me, I don't want to talk to them. Now that I do want to, it's not going to happen, they're going to sense it, and the more they stay away, the more desperate I'll be, and the more desperate the more I'll repel—"

Hannah put her hand on my arm. "Sweetie, you're spiralling. Take a deep breath through the nose." I stared at her. What did that have to do with anything? Hannah rolled her eyes. "Just do it. Go on."

I obeyed, but didn't feel any different.

Hannah nodded. "Good. Now, do it again, but hold the breath when you're full, and then very slowly let it go."

I obeyed, a sense of familiarity appearing in the movement. "That's the exercise the yoga video says to do in the 'good night' video."

"And it works, right?"

I nodded. Those videos helped me get to sleep in under an hour, which I considered a victory given how chatty my brain got at night.

"You feeling better?"

"A bit."

"Well, go talk to people, find out Elliott's alibi, prove your innocence, I don't know, just go do it."

I pulled Hannah in a hug, being careful not to spill my drink on her. "Thank you."

She smiled. "That's what friends are for." She straightened, rotated me a half-turn, and pushed me away from the bar into the room full of people.

I plastered a smile on my face, one that I hoped was more intriguing than demented, and I started walking past people, nodding at them, mouthing what I hoped was an enthusiastic, "Hi."

People were not even acknowledging me. Not a nod, not a smile. How was it that I could lead a workshop with twenty people without breaking a sweat, but when it came to interacting with people in a non-professional environment, I was as socially awkward as a hermit?

"You're here!"

I was pulled into an enthusiastic hug before my brain had a chance to rebel against physical contact with someone I didn't know. I was released, and stared back at Millie's grinning face.

"I had no idea you came to the pub," she said.

I nodded stiffly. "I don't usually come out on weeknights—"

Millie giggled. "I come out every day."

Millie was queer and out? Interesting. "I meant I usually only come down here on a Friday night, and the odd Saturday."

Millie giggled some more. "How sad for your girlfriend."

What? I felt my cheeks burn. Why wasn't it Saturday night when the lights were dimmed? Why did it have to be a weeknight when all the lights were on?

"I meant I usually try to go to bed early on weeknights, because, you know, work the next day."

"Oh, come on Abigail, let your hair down for once."

I swallowed hard and lifted my chin a fraction, not wanting to show her how much her comment had hurt me. I knew I wasn't a fun person. I was always the uptight one, the sensible one. I didn't need to be reminded of it by a colleague, or by anyone really. I didn't need to be reminded that this was how people viewed me.

"Sorry to disappoint," I said icily. "I'm not here for fun."

Millie looked confused. Good. "Why are you at the pub then?"

I looked around, hoping to catch Hannah's eye so she could come to rescue me, but alas she was deep in flirty conversation with what appeared to be a reasonably handsome man. At least I assumed it was flirty, judging by the way she played with her hair, laughed at almost every word he said, and casually put her hand on his forearm as if to say, "stop," but meant, "carry on, I'm loving this."

Without Hannah to help, I was going to have to go through this on my own. I looked around, trying to assess if anyone was eavesdropping, but the people around us seemed to be busy with their own lives, and were not paying us any attention. I supposed it could change if Millie stuck her tongue down my throat. I leaned forward and whispered in her ear. "I'm trying to figure out who Lynn's husband usually hangs out with."

Millie looked confused. "Why?"

"Because I want to know if he has an alibi for the night of her death."

"Isn't it the police's job?"

I gave her a sideways look. Yes it was, but a (big) part of me believed I was smarter than them, and that the only way to clear my name completely was to find the real killer.

"I have my reasons."

"Can I help?"

It was my turn to be thrown. I hadn't expected Millie to offer her help. "Why would you do that? How do you think you can help?"

She wrapped her arms around my waist and pulled me tight against her. I could smell her perfume, sweet and floral, but also sexy.

"In case you haven't noticed, I like you Abigail, I would like to get to know you better, on a personal level." She smiled. "I also know you're not the best with people, whereas I am, so maybe I can get people to talk in front of you, and you can deduce or whatever it is you do."

I did my best to ignore her arms around me, and filed away her declaration that she liked me for when I had two hours to obsess over it, and considered her proposal. It could work, except . . ..

"What if you're the person who killed Lynn?"

Millie's hands fell to her side, and she took a step back. "I'm sorry? What did you say?"

"You had motive, you said so yourself, you hated her."

She stared at me, eyes and mouth wide open. I didn't think I'd ever seen her speechless before.

"How can you say that, no, how can you *think* that? How can you think that I could kill someone?"

"I have to consider all the possibilities, because, like Sherlock Holmes says, 'when you have eliminated the impossible, whatever remains, however improbable, must be the truth'."

"How can you be so cold-hearted," she said, her eyes pooling with tears.

"I'm not cold-hearted, I'm logical."

"Everything all right?" Hannah had snuck up behind me and was giving anxious glances at Millie.

"Yes, just following up on our plan to collect alibis."

Hannah gave me a look that said *what did you do again?* She extended her hand to Millie. "I'm Hannah, Abigail's best friend. Whatever she said to upset you, I'm sure she didn't mean it."

Millie blinked back her tears and shook Hannah's hand. "I'm Millie. I work with Abigail, and she's just accused me of murder."

"I did not," I said. That was just plain offensive. Purely and simply offensive.

Hannah shushed me and turned back to Millie. "Why don't you tell her where you were last Wednesday night, and then Abigail can apologise for accusing you of murder."

I resented the implication that I'd done anything wrong. Why should I apologise? Millie had taken my question the wrong way, and then she'd accused me. *She* should be made to apologise.

* * *

"Fine," Millie said. "I was at the hotel. We had dinner, then we went to the bar, and we stayed until last orders."

"Who's 'we'?" I asked.

"Angela, Beatrice, Charles, and Dave."

All consultants. All people who, as far as I knew, had no specific problem with Lynn.

Millie wiped a tear from her cheek. "Oh, and Jeff too."

The noise levels in the pub were high. "Did you say Jeff? Programme director Jeff?" Millie nodded. That changed things. "He was there the whole time, for dinner and drinks?"

Millie blinked. "Of course he was. But he's . . . you know, old, so he left the bar at about, I don't know, about nine, I guess? Maybe nine thirty? Definitely before ten, because I looked at the clock when the others wanted to do shots and it was exactly ten, and Jeff had already been gone for a while."

I needed to find out what time exactly Lynn had been killed, because it sounded like Jeff had no alibi. The police would have the information, but what were the odds they'd help me? Unless I made it sound like I was trying to help them by providing potentially new information?

"Thank you Millie," I said, "this was very helpful. Enjoy the rest of your night."

I turned away and headed for the other side of the bar. While talking to Millie, I'd spotted a raucous group coming in, led by my favourite food-addiction enablers, Frank and Giuseppe.

"*Cara* Abigail."

I couldn't help smiling every time I saw Giuseppe. I didn't know why, but I felt a strange kinship with him. Maybe it was that we were both part of the LGBTQ+ community. Maybe it was our shared love of pizza, him making them, me eating them. I let him hug me and pressed lightly on his back in a feeble attempt to return the hug.

"I didn't expect to see you here tonight," Giuseppe said, "you don't normally come out during the week."

I let my gaze wander for a few seconds. I was tired of having to repeatedly justify myself for being out tonight, and briefly considered wearing a sign. "I know, but it's been a long day, between work and the police interrogating me again . . . Hannah persuaded me to come out, and I'm glad she did. how come *you're* here?"

Giuseppe smiled. "I left Marco in charge of the restaurant, it's good for him to not always have me around." His smile shifted to a look of concern. "Why did the police interrogate you?"

"Have you not heard?" I was genuinely surprised. In Winburyton, if someone changed underwear brand, the next day, everyone in town knew about it. It was just that kind of place.

Giuseppe furrowed his brow and shook his head. "I guess not. What happened?"

"A woman was pulled out of the pond in the park, you know, the one behind the high street?"

Giuseppe scratched his beard and a moment passed. "But, what does it have to do with you?"

"Well, the woman was my boss on my current project, and because I have been given her job since she disappeared, I'm apparently the police's prime suspect."

Giuseppe pulled me into another hug. "I am so sorry this is happening to you. Is there anything I can do to help?"

I could ask Giuseppe if he knew where Elliott was that night, but something held me back. Maybe because Giuseppe was one of the guys who had the sun tattoo. Objectively, he should be on the potential threatening-note-sender list. Although, if I was honest, the chances of Frank sending the note were higher than Giuseppe's in my opinion. Yes, Lynn had refused his expansion plans, but I just couldn't picture him doing something nasty like that. Besides, Frank might have had a beef with Lynn too.

"Thank you Giuseppe, but I don't think there is, unless you happen to know who killed her and how."

Giuseppe smiled. "I don't even know the woman, I cannot help if you don't tell me her name."

"Duh. Sorry, since everyone seems to know, I assumed you did too, it's Lynn James, the councillor."

"Really? She's dead?" I could see the cogs turning in Giuseppe's head. I could almost hear him wonder how long he should wait before resubmitting his expansion plans to the council. He let go of me and went back to his group of friends. "Did you hear?" he said. "The woman who stopped me expanding the restaurant is dead."

Frank and the others lifted their pints. "May she rest in peace. And good riddance."

"Hear hear," the other men said.

Wow. I hadn't expected that. I knew Lynn wasn't that popular, but she must have been, at some point, to be elected to the council, no?

* * *

Hannah appeared at my side. "So, I got Millie to calm down." She pointed at the group of men toasting. "What's going on there?"

"They're celebrating Lynn's death."

"Seriously?" I nodded. "That's cold."

"I agree. The suspect pool got bigger."

"Are you sure you want to continue?" Hannah sounded worried.

"Continue what? Working the room?

Hannah shook her head. "No, the investigation. What

if you get close to the person who killed her, and they decide to come for you too?"

I cocked my head to the side, thinking. "I could share some of my suspicions with the police, if it makes you feel better, but, honestly, I expect they'll get there first. They're supposed to be trained for this kind of stuff."

"What are you two whispering about?" Frank and greengrocer Sam had flanked us, still looking mighty jolly.

"Nothing interesting," I said. "What about you?"

"Nah, nothing much interesting," Sam said.

"We were just saying it explained why her husband hadn't been out the last few nights," Frank said.

"Is Elliott part of your drinking group then?" Hannah asked.

"Not really," Sam said. "We've all been friends for a long time, of course, but it's more that he's normally sat at the bar and we're sat over here," he said showing the area with the old and uneven tables and the too-low chairs.

"And he's there every night?" I needed to be very careful of not pulling too hard on such a delicate thread or it would break.

"Pretty much," Frank said, "you could almost set your watch on him."

"How so?"

Where had Millie come from? Why was she asking questions to my suspects?

Sam brushed his hair back. "Hel-lo gorgeous. Tell me, what's a pretty little thing like you doing in such a lowbrow establishment?"

I winced so hard I thought I'd pulled a muscle. I cast a sideway glance at Hannah and she appeared to be more amused than pained by Sam's posturing.

Millie didn't seem fazed at all, as if this sort of thing always happened to her.

She gave him a big and slightly flirty smile. "How sweet of you. I'm with some colleagues, and I was a bit bored, so I decided to wander around, and I heard you say something about a man you could set your watch on, and I've never heard that before, so I thought I'd interrupt and ask, then I would go to bed a tiny bit more knowledgeable." She hadn't stopped to catch her breath, not giving Sam (or Frank, who seemed desperate for an in) a chance to get a word in edgewise.

"I'm sure you're plenty smart already," Sam said with a wink, to which Millie responded with a giggle. The noise in the pub seemed to be growing louder with every pint the patrons downed, and I struggled to hear the conversation properly.

Millie delicately placed her hand on Sam's forearm and gave it a light squeeze. "So? Tell me, what does it mean?"

Sam downed his pint. "Haha, I'll tell you, but in a minute, looks like we're out of beer here." He made to move then stopped. "Frank, why don't you come to the bar and help me?"

"What for? Just get a tray," Frank said, eyeing Millie.

"Just come round and help me, you prick."

Frank rolled his eyes and sighed. "Sorry love, looks like the big strong man needs an even bigger and stronger man."

He left and Millie and Hannah burst out laughing.

I looked back and forth between the both of them, but couldn't figure it out. "What? What happened? Why are you laughing?"

"Millie, you're a genius," Hannah said.

Millie? A genius? What was I missing?

"I didn't expect them to bite so fast to be honest," Millie said with a smile.

Hannah pointed at her. "Come on, have you seen yourself? You're gorgeous."

Millie giggled. "Thank you, you're rather pretty yourself."

Hannah beamed at her. "Oh, you're so sweet, thank you."

"Hannah is straight," I interjected. What was this thing I was feeling? I was annoyed at Millie for flirting with Hannah. I was annoyed at Hannah for talking to Millie. I was annoyed that the both of them seemed to get on so well. I was annoyed at being excluded from whatever was going on.

Millie put her hand on my forearm and I felt a tingle under my skin. "It's not like that, don't be jealous Abigail."

Jealous? Me? Wasn't jealousy a primal and unevolved feeling?

"I'm not jealous."

Millie and Abigail exchanged a knowing look before bursting out laughing.

"What? Why are you laughing?"

"It's okay, sweetie" Hannah said, "we love you just the way you are."

I had completely lost the plot. Why were they talking about love and jealousy? What was going on?

Sam and Frank reappeared, carrying three pints each which they handed over to their friends before returning to our little group.

"So," Sam started, "when I said we can almost set our watch by Elliott, I meant just that. For years, day in, day out, he's here every night. He gets in at 7:30 p.m. on the dot, orders a pint of Guinness, goes out for a fag, then returns to this barstool, and stays there, ordering a new pint every twenty minute, until 9:30 p.m. on the dot. Nine-thirty every night, he gets up from the stool, waves goodbye to everyone, and leaves. The same, every night, except Saturday nights, and except for the last three nights. Mind you, if his missus just died, it'd make sense he wouldn't be out at the pub, innit Frank?"

"Makes sense Sam, people might be talking if he was in here, drinking. Mind you, you could argue that it's exactly the time you'd need to get a drink."

"How do you know he wasn't here the last three nights?" I asked.

"Because *we* were, of course."

"All of you?" Millie asked, pointing at their group.

"You bet your sweet ass," Frank said with a wink. "Except for Giuseppe of course, he doesn't close the restaurant until 9:00 p.m. at the earliest, though it's usually more like 10:00 p.m. Some punters don't know when it's time to go home," he said before taking a swig of his beer.

"You mean like you guys?" The barman had just clasped his hands on both their shoulders from behind.

Sam raised his pint at him. "Come on, if we wasn't in here every night, how would this fine establishment survive?" he asked before draining a third of his beer in one go.

The barman laughed. "I'm sure we'd do fine," he called out on his way back to the bar.

"Now ladies, may we interest you in a drink?" Frank asked.

I raised my glass of sparkling water to show it was still three-quarter full. "I'm good, thanks."

Hannah and Millie declined as well, and I moved away from the group. I wanted to go home.

If Lynn had died before nine that Wednesday evening, then they were all in the clear. Jeff, Elliott, Sam, Frank, and the others, they'd all been with people before that time.

After nine though, no one seemed to have an alibi for the night Lynn died. However, only Peter, Jeff, Elliott, and Giuseppe had a motive. And Giuseppe's one didn't seem that strong. She'd refused him planning permission to expand his restaurant a few years ago. So what? He still seemed to do fine, having a full house every night.

31

The office's little kitchen was deserted. That was why I started work early, for the peace and quiet before the daily madness started, the calm before the storm as they said.

"Good morning Abigail," Millie's cheerful voice startled me and I dropped the teabag back into the mug.

"Bugger," I muttered under my breath.

"Why don't you use a spoon," Millie suggested as I went teabag fishing with my fingers. Hot.

"It's quicker this way, usually. Takes much longer to find a damn spoon, then wash it because it will usually be dirty, and dry it because you don't want cold water in your tea. Why do we only have five spoons for an office of nearly a hundred people anyway?"

Millie smiled. "I reckon there were more to start with, and if you did an office sweep, you'd probably find them on people's desks and in drawers."

"Maybe." Maybe if I didn't engage, she'd go away.

"You're not very chatty this morning, are you?"

I grunted, then realised she probably needed to hear words to go away. If only I knew what those words were.

"I'm tired, I went to bed late, in case you didn't notice."

"Late?" Millie sounded genuinely astonished. "We left the pub at like ten. How far do you live?"

"Not far."

"Then you must have been in bed by ten thirty at the latest."

"That's late for me. I need a lot of sleep." *Please go away and let me be in peace*, I silently prayed.

"Listen, last night was fun, I mean, apart from when you accused me of murder obviously."

I quietly brought the mug of tea to my lips. Still too hot. I started blowing on it gently. Her idea of fun and mine really didn't align.

"I was thinking, maybe I can help you investigate?"

I turned around so fast the scalding hot tea sloshed out of the mug onto my shirt and hands, and I dropped the mug. It was going to be one of these days.

"Oh my god, are you all right?" She turned on the kitchen sink's cold water tap on full and forced my hands underneath.

"It's fine." In reality, it hurt like hell, and I wanted to put a cold compress on my chest where the tea had seeped through the fabric, but I wasn't about to admit it. People took advantage if they found your weakness.

"It's not fine." Millie kept my hands firmly under the running cold water. In truth, I wasn't sure what was more painful. The burn from the tea, or the icy cold water. Didn't she know ice could burn too?

After an eternity, Millie turned the water off and handed me a tea towel.

"Do you want me to check out your chest too? You had quite a lot of tea spilling on there."

I felt my cheeks burn and I took a step back. "No. No thanks. I'll . . . I'll just go to the loo and check."

"I didn't mean like that." Millie rolled her eyes. "Jeez. I'm a first aider, that's my job."

I left the mug on the floor and, giving Millie a wide berth, went to the toilets. Safely locked in a cubicle, I unbuttoned my shirt and assessed the damage. The skin was definitely on the red side of pink, but there was no blistering. I'd be fine. I was always fine. I closed the toilet lid and sat on it.

What was I going to do about Millie? About Lynn? About Elliott? I couldn't imagine Shruti giving me any information, and yet, I was so sure it was Elliott. I was never going to get his alibi.

Unless . . . .. I stood up, buttoned up my stained shirt, mildly wincing as the fabric brushed against my scalded skin, and ran back to the kitchen, half expecting Millie to still be there. She was gone, but not before clearing up my mess. The only indication that something had gone wrong were the wads of blue paper scrunched up in the bin.

I marched to her desk, not bothering to acknowledge anyone on the way.

"Millie," I said when I got near. She jumped, and I realised I'd been closer to a shout than a whisper. I lowered my voice. "Sorry, I didn't mean to startle you. Thank you for cleaning up, in the kitchen, I mean. And for helping with my hands. Listen, do you still want to help?" I was speaking much faster than usual, but that only reflected my level of excitement at the idea of having a new lead.

She nodded, slowly, unsure of what she was getting into. She pushed the chair from the desk next to her and swivelled it, a silent invitation for me to sit. "Tell me."

"Not here. Let's get a room."

"I've heard that before," she said, an eyebrow raised.

"What? No. For goodness' sake Millie, I meant a *meeting* room."

I ducked into the first available one, Millie on my heels. "I had an idea." I told her about my loo epiphany. "I can't go back to his office, because he knows me, but *you* could go, he doesn't know you. You could pose as someone who wants to organise an event. Heck, it's not even that far from the truth. You could say you want to organise a team building event to help people accept the change that's coming or whatever it is you do."

Millie sighed

"What?"

"Do you have to insult my work every time we speak?"

"But I didn't."

"You just did. You said, 'or whatever it is I do'."

"Yeah, because I have no idea what kind of witchy thing you do to make people happy about a new system they never wanted in the first place."

"Oh. What am I supposed to do exactly at Elliott's office?"

"I'm hoping his assistant will be there, so you can ask them all about Elliott."

Millie looked dubious. "Or . . . or we could meet that policewoman you talked to in a public, non-police setting, I charm the hell out of her, and she tells us Elliott's alibi."

That would never work. Shruti would never break the rules. I told Millie as much.

"Do you want to bet on it?" Millie replied with a sly smile.

My stomach quivered. She obviously knew something I didn't, but what? I swallowed hard. "What stakes do you have in mind?"

Millie leaned back in the chair, a mischievous smile hovering on her lips. She was enjoying this way too much.

I felt like the mouse about to be fed to a snake. "Let's see," she said, "if I can get Elliott's alibi from the policewoman, you go out with me."

"What do you mean exactly, 'go out'?"

I didn't believe for a second that she would be able to get any information from Shruti, but what if she did? I didn't want to have to be beholden to an unknown bargain. Because, really, semantically, what did 'go out' with someone actually mean?

Technically, I had already gone out with Millie. Once, we left the inside of the office building and went outside to the car park, so we had gone out together. My guess is that she would object to this definition and want to use the more colloquial version of the expression. Hence my request for clarification.

Millie narrowed her eyes at me. "You and I will be going for dinner at a restaurant where we will sit down and share a meal. The length of the meal will be a minimum of one hour long. After dinner, weather permitting, meaning it's not raining or stupidly windy, we will go for a walk for a minimum of thirty minutes where we will be talking about our lives, hopes, and dreams, and will not be talking about work. I will walk you home, and, assuming the date went well, I will kiss you goodnight on the lips and leave."

I stared at her, bewildered. She had thought about this date a lot. I didn't believe for a second she had made this up on the spot. How long had she been thinking about this? I felt ambushed.

" . . . you . . . you will kiss me goodnight . . . on the lips?"

Millie's face turned serious. "Yes, unless you don't want me to?"

I wanted it. I wanted it very much. But there was no way I could admit it. If I did admit it, then she'd know I liked her, and it would make me vulnerable, and she would hurt me. I needed to talk to Hannah. Hannah would know what to do. She was good with people-related conundrums. But I also wanted Elliott's alibi, if it existed. I shut my eyes tight, so tight I started seeing stars against the dark backdrop of my eyelids. "Fine," I said in a sigh.

I reopened my eyes, and Millie looked less than happy. Why? I'd just agreed to her terms, she should have been ecstatic.

"I appear to have misread the situation," she said coldly. "I'll get the information you want from that policewoman, but don't worry, I won't force you to go on a date with me."

"Oh." I was disappointed. Why would she talk about going on a date, and then take it back? Humans were so confusing.

32

I'd been panicking over my bargain with Millie all weekend, her help in exchange for a date, and now here we were.

"Are you sure we should be doing this?" I asked her. "Isn't it against the law?"

Millie wiped the inside of her windscreen with a chamois pad, trying to clear the fog that our breaths had created. We'd both been sat in her car for thirty minutes in the car park across the street from the police station, waiting for Shruti to come out. It had been Millie's idea. She'd pointed out that she needed to be sure of the woman she was supposed to talk to, having only caught a glimpse of her outside the project office once.

"It's fine," Millie said. "I just need to be sure."

"But . . . isn't it like stalking?"

"I'm not trying to find out anything about her life, and I'm not trying to harm her, so I'm pretty sure we're fine. At worst, we're loitering."

"What if someone asks us what we're doing here, what we're waiting for?"

"Then I'll kiss you," Millie said, completely unfazed, "and they'll see us as two lovers making out, and they'll leave us alone."

A part of me hoped someone would come and ask what we were doing here.

Another part, the sensible one, reminded me that I jumped in new relationships too fast, and that the person I was dating always ended up being different, because I projected what I wanted this person to be, and ignored who they were for real.

Someone came out of the police station. I straightened up in my seat while trying to keep my head down—like a bird, no neck and head way misaligned with the body. My yoga teacher would have a fit.

"That's her," I said.

Millie fixed her eyes on the woman coming through the doors of the police station, and heading away on foot. "You're sure?"

"Of course I'm sure. Why would I say it was her if I wasn't sure?" What was wrong with Millie? Why did she keep on doubting everything I said? Didn't she know I was always right?

"Alright, don't get on your high horse," Millie said, "but do get out of my car."

"What?"

Millie sighed. I could only see the side of her head, but I knew she had just rolled her eyes at me.

"I cannot have you in the car watching me while I'm trying to find the information you need. You're going to cramp my style. So get out, but don't slam the door."

"Why not?"

Millie made a sound between a whine and a grunt, a sound that wouldn't have been inappropriate in her own bathroom, after a heavy meal lacking in fibre, but I couldn't understand why she would make it here and now.

"Because if you slam the door, she's going to hear it, she might look around to see where the sound is coming from, then she'll spot you coming out of my car, and I won't get the teeniest shot at asking her anything without her becoming immediately suspicious. So get out, now, and go home."

I did as she asked. Face frozen in disdain, hoping it would be enough to stop my lower lip from trembling as I fought back tears. Why would Millie suddenly be so mean?

As I walked away from the car, I realised Shruti was walking in the same direction as I was, and that if I went home the normal way, it would look like I was following her. I turned around and headed the opposite way. I could take the next turn, walk up the crazy high hill that was bordered by these gorgeous Victorian houses, and turn left to head back in the normal direction, but on a path parallel to Shruti's.

It started drizzling, and I kicked myself for not taking my folding umbrella that morning. The weather forecast had shown clear blue skies for the whole day, with only ten percent chance of rain. I lifted my coat's collar, a feeble attempt to guard against the cold mist and strode away.

The hill was steep and I slowed down as I ran out of breath. Some of the houses were truly gorgeous, with their original brick porch archways, and wisterias climbing up them, but others were a living embodiment of what not to do when renovating a period house. They'd removed the individual wooden sash windows from the bow window, and had replaced the front ones by an extra-large uPVC window, making it look like as if it was a shopfront.

I stopped at the top of the hill and leaned against a low brick wall. I needed to catch my breath, just for a minute. The street was dark, in spite of the lampposts placed at regular intervals, and it was quiet. Everybody living here was either already home getting dinner ready, or wouldn't be coming home from a hard day's work in London for another hour or so. This was the golden time, when nothing happened, and everything was peaceful.

Across the street, a front door opened on one of the old and unrestored houses, letting a sliver of light spill out of the hallway. A man came out, paused under the porch, looked around, up and down the street, as if checking for something or someone. Instinctively, I crouched low on the ground. I wasn't sure why I wanted to stay out of sight, but my instinct said to not show myself, to not let the man see me.

The man buttoned his coat all the way up and went to close the front door behind him when a hand emerged from the gap and grabbed his forearm, stopping him. I shuffled to get a better view of the person inside, but a car parked in front of the house partially blocked my view. The man turned around and leaned forward inside the house, seemingly giving a goodbye kiss to whomever was inside. It was definitely not his wife, a goodbye kiss to a spouse was more like a two seconds' peck on the lips. This kiss was going on forever.

The man finally leaned back, the door shut behind the man, and he headed for the short gate closing the small front garden. When the street's lamppost light fell on his face, it took all my self-control to not gasp audibly.

33

"And you're sure it was him?" Hannah asked for the third time.

"Yes," I repeated, annoyed at her insistence. "I'm a hundred percent sure it was Elliott. I saw his face when he walked under the lamppost. It was definitely him."

"And he was kissing someone."

"Yes!" Honestly, Hannah could be so frustrating sometimes. I was right, I knew it, she knew it, so why did she keep on asking the same question?

"That's interesting . . . I mean, I know Lynn said she thought her husband was having an affair, but it's weird to have confirmation."

"Why?"

Hannah's tea sloshed in the mug as she tried to emphasise her point. "I don't know, from what you said about him, he doesn't seem the type."

I guess I could see her point. Elliott, the one time I'd spoken to him, had seemed very unassuming, quiet, not the kind of guy to make waves. Looking at it from the other side though, Lynn being away three to four nights a week for years would have allowed him to have more than an affair, he could have been having a double life, and no one would have known about it. Maybe the stress of having to sneak around, what with Lynn back home every night for the past three months had been too much, and he'd snapped.

"Do you think I should tell the police?" I asked. Hannah frowned in incomprehension. "I mean, I know his lover's address now, that seems like a concrete enough proof, don't you think?"

"Maybe." Hannah seemed really hesitant. "All you really have is proof he's having an affair now, not proof he has been having an affair for years, even if Lynn had her suspicions a few months ago, and it's definitely not proof he killed his wife."

I hated it when she was right.

34

Tail between my legs, I walked home. What had seemed like a big breakthrough had now turned into another anecdotal fact. Maybe I could snoop around, to find out who lived in the house. Or I could stake it out. If I sat in the back seat of my car, and put a woollen hat on or something, I could probably be near invisible.

I had almost reached the entrance to my block of flats, head down to guard against the mist that had upgraded to a drizzle, when I walked into someone wearing bright yellow rain boots.

"Sorry," I muttered before stepping out of their way.

"Abigail."

I lifted my head and stared. "Millie? What are you doing here?"

"I thought you might want to know how I did with Detective Sergeant Shruti Anand?"

I did want to know, but a part of me also didn't, because I knew myself. I knew I would want Millie to tell me how she got the information, and my instinct told me she'd flirted, and maybe more, and I didn't like the idea of her kissing Shruti. Or kissing anyone really.

We paused in the entrance hall for a minute, me checking the mailbox, Millie shaking the water from her coat.

"How did you know where I lived?" While Millie didn't give off creepy stalker vibes, I was pretty sure I hadn't given her my address.

A flush crept up from her neck to the root of her hair, painfully obvious under the harsh neon lighting from the entrance hall. She looked down, appearing highly preoccupied with shaking water off from the bottom of her coat.

"Hannah."

Hannah? My Hannah? My best friend? My now ex-best friend. The traitor.

I considered asking her for more details when I noticed the water dripping from her hair, and her teeth chattering. I never really had anyone in my apartment before, apart from Hannah, and the odd plumber or electrician, and more recently, the police. I didn't like the idea of people, in general, in my flat, and I liked the idea of a colleague, specifically, in my flat even less, but I couldn't decently let her catch her death.

"Come on," I said. "Let's go up, I'll make you a cup of tea."

Millie nodded, not bothering (or unable?) to reply.

I unlocked my front door and pushed it open. "Would you mind taking your boots off?" I asked.

"Why?"

"Because there are no shoes in the house," I said. Wasn't it obvious?

"Why? That's a weird rule."

"I like it when the flat is clean, but I hate cleaning. Keeping shoes on drags dirt from the outside all over the apartment, and on days like today, water, and mud, so there are no shoes in the flat. I know it sounded like I was asking, and how that could be confusing, but I was just trying to be polite. If you don't want to take your boots off, we'll have to talk out in the hall."

Millie's lips parted, showing a hint of her slightly crooked teeth. Shaking her head, she pulled her first boot off. "Are you seriously for real? You're unbelievable!"

"Err . . . thank you?"

"It wasn't a compliment Abigail!"

"Oh." What was it then? Why was she so unhappy? I left her to struggle with her second boot, ignored Jasper-the-wuss that dove under the sofa, and padded out to the bathroom, returning with a couple of towels.

"Here," I said handing Millie one, "you can dry your hair while I make tea."

"Why?" Millie asked aggressively. "Are you worried I'm going to drip all over your floors and furniture?"

Huh? "No, I just thought your wet hair might make you feel cold. How do you take your tea?"

"Actually, do you have hot chocolate by any chance? I'm not a big tea fan, and it's a bit late for coffee."

"I only have this weird instant rose-flavoured chocolate . . . it was a gift," I added. No way would I have bought this myself, but I'd been taught it was bad form to decline an unwanted present. "I think I have decaf coffee if you prefer."

"No, it's fine, I'll try the chocolate. I like trying weird things," she added with a teasing tone in her voice I couldn't quite figure out.

"Have you lived here long then?" Millie called out from the living room.

"About eight years," I said as I poured the hot water on the chocolate powder and stirred like a maniac. "I was renting another flat in the building for two years before that, then this one came up for sale and it was a little bit better than mine, so I bought it."

"Must be nice," Millie said.

I put the mug of steaming hot chocolate in front of her and the milk bottle next to it. "What's that?"

"To be able to just buy a flat when it comes up."

I fought the outrage rising in me and did my best to keep my tone even. "Of course it's nice, but it didn't just happen."

Millie stirred some cold milk in her mug and brought it to her full and very kissable lips. "How so? Didn't you ask your parents for the deposit?"

* * *

Mug of tea in hand, I burst out laughing.

"Careful," Millie said, "you're going to burn yourself again."

I held my breath in an effort to keep my hilarity at bay and carefully set the mug on a coaster.

"What was so funny?" Millie asked.

"I'm sorry, it's just I pictured my parents' faces if I went to ask them for money, or anything really. The whole idea is just so ridiculous. Thank you though, I hadn't laughed this much in ages. Feels good."

Millie hung her head, probably in an effort to hide the flush creeping up her cheeks. "A lot of people your age buy their first place thanks to the bank of mum and dad, so I assumed . . .."

"No, this flat is the result of me basically not doing or buying anything for the two years I rented. Plus working hard, so I got promoted twice in two years, with the pay rises that came with it."

Millie looked doubtful. "Yeah, but . . . you still need a lot of money to put a deposit together, especially for your first place."

She was annoying me now, again. "It really all adds up. Nights out at the pub, takeaways, sandwiches for lunch from the supermarket, going to the cinema, taking a taxi somewhere rather than walking or taking the bus, buying another pair of shoes I don't actually need. I cut all of that out for two years, and saved enough for a deposit on this flat."

"But . . . you're not living. You're surviving." Millie sounded extremely concerned.

"How so?"

"If all you're doing is working and sleeping. And preparing your lunch."

I smiled. "Yes, for two years I cut back on a lot of things. But that didn't stop me from taking the train up to London on a weekend, which didn't cost me anything, since I had my season ticket for work anyway, and went to a market in the morning, and to a museum in the afternoon. I did that about once a month. It didn't stop me from meeting friends and going for walks. It didn't stop me from buying nice fresh food to cook at home, rather than buying greasy and expensive takeaways. I still went on holiday abroad once a year, but I booked my flights and hotel at least six months in advance. I still went to the pub, but drank only sparkling water, and no more than three a night, and only one night a week."

"But that's crazy. Who lives like that?"

"If you want something bad enough, then you're willing to make sacrifices for it. And to be honest, it really didn't feel like that much of a sacrifice, and it was only for two years."

"Really? Why only two years?"

"Because it was just so I could save up enough for a deposit. The mortgage on this place is only fifty pounds a month more than what I used to pay in rent. And my salary has gone up in the last eight years."

"But what gave you the idea? It would never have occurred to me that all those little things cost so much."

"It's just the way I was educated. Now, can we talk about something else please? Did you learn anything from Shruti?" It was, after all, the reason why Millie was in my flat.

Millie looked like she was about to push me on my money strategy, but thankfully dropped the subject. "Fine. Peter has an alibi, he was already back up north where he lives, and, even though he apparently burst out laughing and told Shruti it was the best news of the year, he'd gone to his local that night and bought his rounds with a card, so definitely not him."

"Bugger. I didn't really think it was him, but still."

"It looks like Lynn was having an affair, but they haven't been able to find who with, so that seems a bit of a dead end, at least for now."

I nodded. I didn't want to tell Millie about my suspicions about Jeff, not unless there was a reason to.

"God, you're killing me."

"I've heard that before," Millie said with her annoyingly teasing smile. "Fine. Elliott gave an alibi that fell apart the minute the police started verifying it."

"So he lied, and he doesn't have an alibi?"

"Looks that way. Does it matter? Does he have a motive of some sort?"

"I'd think so. After I left your car, I walked back to town a different way so Shruti wouldn't see me, and I saw Elliott kissing someone."

"Who?"

"Don't know, I didn't see."

"You have to tell Shruti. If he has the motive and the opportunity, that's two out of three. And since they lived together, I'd think he definitely had the means."

"Hmm." I didn't know if it was because Shruti had interrogated me twice, or because she'd made me feel like I'd done something wrong, but I didn't want to tell her. Especially if I was wrong, then I'd look like a complete idiot.

"It's the right thing to do, you know that. If you don't tell her, Elliott might get away with it, do you really want that on your conscience? Do I have to persuade you, the way I persuaded Shruti?"

"How *did* you persuade Shruti?" That had been bothering me more than I cared to admit.

Millie shifted uncomfortably in her seat and blushed. "Maybe I'll tell you, one day."

Translation, whatever she'd done, I'd find objectionable.

35

I waited until seven the next morning to text Shruti. I hadn't wanted to risk waking her, and was surprised she texted right back. Who was coherent enough at seven to pick up their work phones, read, *and* reply to texts? I knew *I* was, but everyone else I knew was still gulping their first coffee at that time.

Shruti had said she'd be at the station after 7:30 a.m., so I messaged Sybil to ask her to reschedule my first two meetings of the day and popped in on my way to work, unable to shake the unfounded feeling that I was playing hooky.

Shruti came to greet me at the front counter, two steaming hot goblets in hand. "Morning, Abigail." She handed me a goblet. "Tea?" I nodded. "I would have offered you coffee, but frankly what we get out of the machine here is closer to sludge than coffee. Tea is the least objectionable option as my brother would say."

"Tea is fine, thank you."

I followed her through the now familiar corridors into an interview room.

"So, what was so urgent?" Shruti asked as she closed the door.

I shifted in my seat. I hadn't bothered taking my coat off, as I wasn't planning on staying long, but I was regretting it. "It's not urgent as such, it's just that it feels important.

Elliott James was cheating on his wife. I saw him kiss someone last night."

Shruti sat down and leaned forward against the table. "Last night? What time was that?"

"Between 6:30 p.m. and 7:00 p.m., I guess. Does it matter?"

"And you're sure it was Elliott James?"

I hated that she answered my questions with more questions. "Yes, I am, I saw his face clearly under the lamppost. Listen, that's not the point. The point is that he has multiple motives to kill his wife, since he's having an affair, and his business isn't doing well, he doesn't seem to have an alibi, since his friends told me he wasn't at the pub that night for the first time in years, and he almost certainly had the means. He could just have taken Lynn for a romantic walk near the pond and killed her."

Shruti suddenly looked very tired. In my rush to go in earlier, I hadn't noticed, but now I could see the heavy bags under her eyes, the hair that was only partially brushed and hurriedly tied back at the nape of her neck rather than gathered in a neat, low bun as usual.

It was so obvious I could have kicked myself. "Elliott's dead isn't he?"

Shruti's eyes momentarily widened in surprise then she relaxed back into her seat. "I'd ask how you know, but I'm guessing it would involve a lengthy explanation that would make perfect sense on how you picked up on small details that led you to a logical conclusion?"

"Err . . . yes, but I was only fifty percent sure. What happened?"

"Stabbed and thrown into the pond, very similar to his wife. Probably the same killer. Do you have any thoughts on that?"

I shook my head. I'd been so sure Elliott had killed Lynn, and it turned out I'd been right all along: I was a complete idiot who had no business detectiving.

36

When I got to the office, I dove straight in my first meeting, then the next one and the next one, never even getting a chance to sit behind my own desk. When I finally got a thirty minutes' gap in my calendar at 12:30 p.m., I didn't hesitate. I took my lunchbox from the shared fridge and dove into my car. I was parked far from the office entrance, owing to the fact the spots were first come, first served, and I had been one of the last to arrive onsite. It had been annoying when I was running late this morning, but now I was grateful for the relative seclusion that would award me thirty minutes of peace and quiet.

I sat in the passenger seat and pushed it all the way back. Why dine behind the wheel in a cramped space, when I could be very comfortable on the passenger side? I laid down a tea towel on the dashboard, and started pulling out today's lunch: Ploughman sandwich with a no-salad salad. It was, for all intent and purposes, a salad, but didn't contain any green leaves. Dessert was going to be an apple and a small bar of German chocolate, but I could eat those in a meeting later if I ran out of time.

I turned on the radio to a classical music station, leaned back in my seat and took a deep breath. "Aaah," I exhaled audibly. Finally alone.

I unclipped the lid from my salad container, dug my fork in and put it to my lips when someone rapped on the driver's side window, scaring the beejeezus out of me, and sending the content of the fork flying all over the car.

"Why?" I yelled at the familiar face through the closed window. "Why would you do that?"

I put my salad down and got out of the car. "Seriously Millie, is it too much to ask to be left alone for thirty tiny little minutes to eat my lunch in peace? I'm going to have to get the car cleaned because of you."

Millie's face had turned from grinning to blank through my tirade. She squared her shoulders, turned on her heels, and walked away without a word.

"So that's all it was," I yelled after her, "just a stupid prank? Let's scare Abigail and see how much of her lunch gets stuck to the car ceiling?" I was fighting tears now, and no idea where they came from, I just knew I couldn't let them win. I was a master of my emotions, I repeated to myself like a mantra. "You're all the same," I yelled before sitting back in the car.

My voice had broken, but Millie had already turned the corner, so I was quite confident that she hadn't heard me at all, and that, even if she had heard me, she would have been too far to pick up on my voice breaking. I tried to pick up the bits of rice, peas, cheese, pumpkin seeds, and other assorted goodies from the upholstery but it was no good, the vinaigrette had already spread and left its greasy mark everywhere.

I'd need to find some paper to sit on tonight if I didn't want to stain my trousers too. It was going to cost me a fortune to get it cleaned, no doubt my regular spot wouldn't be able to cope with embedded grease.

The driver's door was wrenched open and Millie sat down.

"Noooo," I yelled.

"So, now we can't even have a private conversation? Just because I scared you by accident?" She shook her head and made to leave. "Forget it. You're nuts."

"I'm not," I protested. "I was trying to stop you from sitting in greasy salad dressing. You've probably got stains on the back of your dress now."

Millie got out of the car and contorted herself to assess the damage. I had a good view from where I sat, and I was enjoying her curves while feeling guilty about the stains on a dress I'd never seen her wear before.

"Bugger," she said as she spotted the darker red blotches. "This dress is dry clean-only."

"Why would you buy a dry clean-only dress?"

Millie sat back in the driver's seat and shut the door. "It was pretty."

I pointed at the seat. "But, why . . .?"

Millie shrugged. "Whether the dry cleaner's needs to remove one or five grease stains doesn't make a difference, he's still going to charge me extra."

I took a mouthful of my salad and chewed slowly. "I'm shorry," I said while swallowing. "I shouldn't have yelled at you."

"No you shouldn't have. But I'm sorry too, for scaring you, it wasn't my intention."

"What was your intention then?" I shovelled a couple more bites of the salad in my mouth. Damn I was hungry.

"I wanted to check you had told Shruti about Elliott's mistress."

I held my fork mid-air, frozen. Shruti hadn't told me to keep Elliott's death quiet, but I assumed it was implied, and I hadn't told Hannah about it. I hadn't seen Millie all morning, so even if I'd wanted to, I wouldn't have been able to. But what now? Should I tell her or not?

I'd start with the truth and see where that would lead me.

"I did. I went to see her on my way to work this morning. That's why I was a bit late. Or later than normal. I wasn't technically late, I was still in before Sunrise."

"Okay." Millie put her hand on my arm and a shiver coursed through my body. "I don't know why you are panicking, because you have no reason to. I'm not going to be angry with you if you didn't tell Shruti, I'll just be a bit disappointed, because you promised, and I'll badger you until you tell her, but I'm definitely not angry."

"It's not that. I did tell her about Elliott's motives, and the means, and the fact he wasn't at the pub that night, and I pointed out that he probably had the opportunity."

"And what did she say?"

"I don't know if I can tell—"

"Why couldn't you tell me?"

"I wasn't . . . it's not . . . The problem is not you, the problem is everyone. I don't know if I'm allowed to tell anyone." My phone buzzed with a number I didn't recognise. I let it go to voicemail, I still had fifteen minutes of me-time, and I intended to use them. While I was getting to the bottom of my salad, I still had my sandwich to eat.

"What did Shruti say to you that could be confidential?" Millie asked.

I knew she thought I was lying, the tone of her voice left little doubt, but what if I wasn't supposed to tell anyone and I did. Would they send me to jail?

My phone buzzed again and I rejected the call. Seconds later, it was starting again.

"Someone really want to reach you," Millie observed.

"It's my work phone," I said carefully, not wanting to splutter any of my sandwich on her or the car.

"Whoever is calling me, they want me to do work, or think about work. I still have just over ten minutes free before an afternoon marathon of meetings, and I intend to enjoy them."

The phone buzzed again and we both stared at it. "How about I pick up," Millie offered, "and I'll tell them to send you an email because you're not available."

"Whatever they say, do not pass me the phone, I'm begging you."

Millie extended her arm to get the vibrating piece of plastic and brought it up to her ear. "Hello, Abigail's phone, Millie speaking." She listened to the other side and shot me a glance.

"No no no no no," I mouthed while making throat cutting gestures with my hand. I wasn't there for anyone.

"I'll pass on the message." Millie hung up and put the phone back on the dashboard.

"Do I even want to know?" I asked, cringing.

"Probably. It was Hannah. She said, and I quote, 'pick up your fudging phone goddamit'."

* * *

"Hannah? Why would she call me on my work phone?"

Millie rolled her eyes. "I'm going to go out on a limb and say it was because you didn't pick up your personal one?"

I swallowed the last bite of my sandwich whole and wiped my fingers on the tea towel. I rooted through my messenger bag and extracted my phone. Thirty-eight missed calls from Hannah. Five text messages. I showed the screen to Millie and started poking at the screen to call Hannah back. No point in reading the texts or checking for voicemails. "I wonder what happened that she would call so many times," I muttered.

"Finally," Hannah's voice on the other side of the line yelled in my ear. I winced and moved the phone away from my ear as far as I could in the confined space of the car, but I could still hear her yelling.

"Hannah, stop yelling at me and tell me what's going on."

"It's going on that Lynn's husband is dead, that's what's going on."

"Oh. How do you know?"

"Is that really all you have to say?!"

"Hannah, humour me, how do you know?"

"It popped up on the Winburyton chronicles website an hour ago. Which you would have known if you'd bothered picking up your phone, or reading your texts."

"I'm sorry my lovely, it's been a busy morning."

"Whatever. Why aren't you freaking out?"

I chewed on my lower lip. "I already knew."

"What? How? You—"

"Listen Hannah, I love you, but I'm going to have to go. I'll see you tonight, okay?"

"Fine." Hannah hung up.

"Everything okay?" Millie asked. "There was a lot of yelling."

"Yeah, sorry about that. Anyway, that actually answered my previous question, and I guess I can tell you since it's now all over the internet."

"What?"

"Elliott's dead."

"What? How?"

"I don't have details, just that they found him in the same pond they found Lynn."

"Did he kill himself?" Millie seemed mildly in shock.

"Not unless he stabbed himself and stumbled into the pond."

"Shit. So who killed Lynn then?"

"I don't know, and to be honest, I think it's time for me to acknowledge that I'm no detective. I'd been so sure it was Elliott, and now someone's killed him, probably the same person who killed Lynn, given that both bodies were dumped in the same place."

Millie cradled my face in her hands and put her forehead against mine. An incredibly intimate gesture, but I didn't want her to let go. "You are an awesome detective, Abigail."

"Thank you. I don't believe you though."

"Shut up." Millie looked at her phone. "I should get back, I've got a meeting at one o'clock."

"I have one too." I hesitated. What if she thought I was too forward? "Do you want to walk back together?"

"Sure, that'd be nice."

We took a couple of steps in silence before I remembered. "Why did you come to my car?"

Millie gave me a teasing smile. "To remind you I got Shruti to tell me about Elliott's alibi. Not that it matters anymore," she added with a touch of sadness in her voice.

"And?"

"And I came to collect on our bet."

The date. I'd forgotten about this. Or, more exactly, I'd chosen to not remember it. If I ignored it, then it wouldn't happen.

"Abigail, be honest." The seriousness in Millie's tone surprised me. I'd heard her flirty, amused, giggly, playful, but I couldn't recall a time I'd heard her so serious. "Do you like me?"

Why did she keep asking me such tough questions?

"I . . . don't know. I guess," I muttered. I sounded so lame, but she was asking me to put myself out there naked, and I didn't know how to do that. Vulnerability meant hurt and pain, that's what I'd experienced the whole time growing up. Anything resembling emotions would lead my parents to chorus for me to toughen up. I'd obeyed, like the good girl I was who just wanted her parents to love her.

Millie nodded. "It's fine. I'll take that, for now. However, I'm serious about the date. You owe me one, but I'll make a small change to the terms of our bet. I won't make you go out on a date I've planned."

I was so confused. "Really? Why?"

"Because, now, as per the new terms, you will ask me out when you are ready to ask me out. You have a week."

"A week?"

"You like deadlines, facts, black and white. I'm giving you a deadline."

I hung my head down. She knew me well, better than I'd expected. I lifted my head and looked her in the eyes. "It's a deal. Just don't expect too much from me, please."

37

Mid-afternoon, I'd escaped from the office to get supplies for my catch-up with Hannah.

"Have you heard about poor Leo?" Frank asked before pointing at the slab of Emmental cheese on the scales. "Is that too big?"

"That's fine, it's mostly holes anyway. Who's Leo?"

Frank wrapped the cheese and added it to the small pile on the counter. "Elliott. Elliott James. Didn't you know him?"

"I only met him once, I knew his wife more. Sort of. Why do you call him Leo? That's not really a standard nickname for Elliott, is it?"

Frank laughed a small, pained laugh. "Yeah, I guess it's not. It's because of Giuseppe."

Huh? What did Giuseppe have anything to do with it?

Frank carried on. "When he got here from Italy, in year twelve, his English wasn't that good, probably as good as my GCSE French was, and I got a C in French. Anyway. Long story short, we kind of all became friends, but he couldn't say Elliott very well, he kept on detaching the syllables, like ey-lee-o-tt. Eventually we stopped correcting him, and 'Leo' stuck as Elliott's nickname ever since."

Something was giving me a brain itch, but I couldn't figure out what. "Remind me, who was in that little group?"

"Sam, Giuseppe, Leo, Nick, Aaron, and myself obviously. Why?"

I almost had it. "Nick and Aaron were at the pub last week, right?"

"Love, you're going to need to be more specific."

I raised an eyebrow. "The night Sam and you were trying to hit on Millie, the very pretty woman who was with Hannah and me."

"Yeah sure. Weren't they both trying to go after the new barmaid that night?"

I nodded. I remembered, but my brain was still itching. I paid Frank, and put the cheese in my shopping bag. "Thank you so much Frank, you've been very helpful."

Frank scratched his head. "I have? How so?"

I grinned at him. "With your knowledge of cheeses, of course."

As I left the shop, Hannah texted.

Hannah: i have news

I paused for a second to run through the scenarios. If I replied now, I was guaranteed to be late for the meeting with all the workstream leads. No one had told me to investigate either Lynn's or Elliott's death. Not finding out who killed them wouldn't make me look bad. Being late to the meeting would.

I jumped in the car and hurried back to the office.

* * *

Once I'd parked the car in a spot that was even further from the entrance than in the morning, I only had four minutes before the meeting.

Walking fast, I texted Hannah back. Phones and I were not friends. Texting, while inconvenient when attempting to walk fast, was friendlier to my brain.

Me: Can I invite Millie to our catch-up at yours tonight please?

Hannah: do i know her

Me: She thought I'd accused her of murder that night at the pub. Very pretty.

Hannah: sure shes fun

I swiped in, ran up the stairs, practically threw the bag containing the cheese in the fridge, and launched myself in the meeting room where all the workstream leads had assembled. No laptop, no notebook, but at least, I was (just) on time.

<h1 style="text-align:center">38</h1>

Hannah's kitchen table was littered with printouts. "What are these?"

"Screenshots. I found Elliott's company's Facebook page."

My jaw dropped. I felt it. "How?"

"By accident. I searched for his company online, just in case we'd missed something when we first looked him up, and I missed the space between 'Spectrum' and 'Vox'. Turns out, he made the same typo on his Facebook page."

The bell rung at the door. "It must be Millie," I said. "I'll get it."

I re-introduced Millie and Hannah, and we sat down at the kitchen table.

"I don't mean to be rude," Millie said, "but I don't have much time, I told the others I'd meet them at that pizza restaurant at seven. Why did you want me here?"

"Well," I said, "since you've been helping with the investigation into Lynn's disappearance, I thought it would be nice to invite you to our regular catch-up?"

Millie beamed at us. "That's very thoughtful of you Abigail, thank you. And thank you Hannah, for having me in your home."

I zoned out while Hannah and Millie were going back and forth with the thank-yous, and scanned through some of the printouts of the events' company's Facebook page. Elliott being dead meant I had no idea who had killed Lynn, but you never knew, someone might have commented 'I'll kill you and your wife' on one of the posts.

The problem with looking at paper rather than a screen was that you couldn't expand the comments or see the names of the people who had liked or shared each post.

"I need to look at this on a screen."

Hannah went for her laptop—which, thankfully, was already on—and we crowded around the small screen. Methodically, I clicked on each post and expanded comments and likes.

Millie pointed at the screen. "This guy seems to be sharing every single one of Elliott's company's posts."

"Makes sense," I said, "that's Giuseppe, the guy who owns the pizza restaurant." Millie nodded. "Elliott and he have been friends since they were seventeen. Friends support each other in any way they can."

Hannah clicked on Giuseppe's name and we landed on his profile. "Oops, sorry, didn't mean to do that."

She was about to hit the back button when I stopped her. "Hang on a second."

I scrolled through Giuseppe's posts. "Look, a certain 'Leo' hearted pretty much all of them."

"So? That's probably his boyfriend?" Hannah said. "Look, he sent him cute memes too."

The neurons in my brain fired up and a wave of nausea hit me. "I think it's Elliott. Frank told me 'Leo' was Elliott's nickname."

"No way," Hannah said, "Elliott was married, to a woman, your boss."

"So?" Millie asked. "That doesn't mean anything."

I clicked on 'Leo' and his profile came up.

"Not much to see there," Millie said. "Just his birthday."

Hannah pulled a couple of printouts. "I saw Elliott's date of birth on the Company's House stuff. Here it is." She put the sheet of paper next to the screen. "Same month, same year. It has to be Elliott. Elliott is this 'Leo' guy."

"Elliott and Giuseppe? Together?" I hadn't seen this one coming, not even a little bit.

"Even if they were having a secret affair, it doesn't mean anything," Hannah said.

Her voice had wavered, as if she was trying to convince herself it wasn't true, rather than stating a fact.

"If Giuseppe was in love with Elliott, why would he have killed him?" Millie said.

I stared at the screen. If Giuseppe and Elliott were together, where did Lynn fit in in that equation? And if both of them had affairs, why were they still together up till the moment they died? Why didn't they just get a divorce? Humans were puzzling.

I was turning the facts around in my head, doing my best to ignore the grating sound of the wall clock ticking away the seconds.

My brain had been itching since my meeting with Frank that afternoon, and it finally came to me.

"The note."

"What note?" Millie asked.

Hannah kindly explained about the note Lynn had received, which was how I'd gotten tangled into this mess.

"The note Lynn had received was addressed to 'L.' James. It read, 'Tell the truth or I will'," I said. "What if it was meant for Elliott, *Leo*, instead of Lynn?"

"Like Giuseppe threatening Elliott?" Hannah asked. "But why? Why not send him a text, or an email, or going to see him at the office?"

We fell back into silence. To keep my hands busy rather

than to fill my stomach, I tore a piece of salt-and-pepper baguette, and spread a young and very fresh goat's cheese. It was so creamy I probably should have used a spoon over a knife.

"Maybe they were on a break, except Giuseppe didn't want to be?" Millie suggested.

Mouth still full, I nodded. Giuseppe had never struck me as particularly possessive, but the only people who knew what was really going on in a relationship where the people who were in it.

"So he sent the note, threatening to tell the truth, presumably to Lynn, about Elliott cheating—" Hannah said.

"But Elliott never got the note, since Lynn involuntarily intercepted it, believing it was for her," I said. The pieces of the puzzle clicking together were giving me an incredible rush. Why would people do drugs when they could do this?

A lightbulb turned on in my head. "The second note."

"What second note?" Millie asked.

"The night Lynn disappeared, she left a voicemail saying she'd received a second note, but she didn't say what was in the note. What if it was a time and place?"

"Okay," Hannah said, "so she went, something happened and she died, but if Giuseppe loved Elliott, why kill him?"

I started thinking out loud. "Maybe he told Elliott what he did? Or maybe he told Elliott that now he was a widower, they could be together properly, be seen out in public together, and Elliott freaked out? Maybe he got violent and Giuseppe defended himself?"

"We don't have any proof."

I chewed on my lip. Millie was right, we didn't.

"I think you should tell Shruti. Maybe they found evidence on Elliott's body that could tie him to the killer, whoever it is," Hannah said.

I didn't want to believe that Giuseppe, our Giuseppe, could have done something so horrific as murder, but Lynn's and Elliott's lives had been mostly separate for such a long time, I couldn't think of anyone else who would have wanted *both* of them dead.

"Ok, let's take it to Shruti."

39

Millie had gone over to Giuseppe's restaurant to meet with the consultants who'd selected it as tonight's feeding station, and she'd taken Hannah along with her. Whatever happened with Shruti, we'd agreed I'd go meet them there afterwards. And if Shruti didn't think Giuseppe was guilty, I would try to talk to Giuseppe after dinner.

I'd walked in the police station with a weight in my stomach. I knew sharing what we'd found was the right thing to do, but it didn't mean I liked it.

Not even five minutes later, Shruti and DC Robins were escorting me out.

"Never heard such a ridiculous theory," DC Robins grumbled. "Giuseppe Rossi is a pillar of our community."

I struggled to navigate the mixed emotions I was feeling. On the one hand, I was relieved. I'd shared my suspicions, and they'd been quashed. Duty done. On the other hand, I felt like they'd barely listened.

"At least tell me this," I said. "Does Giuseppe have an alibi for the nights Lynn James and Elliott James were killed?"

Shruti and DC Robins exchanged a glance.

"You didn't check, did you?" I said.

DC Robins puffed up his chest. "We had no reason to ask for Mr Rossi's alibi, he was never a suspect. He had no reason to want either Mrs or Mr James dead."

I wanted to bang my head against a wall. It wasn't just a feeling after all. Neither of them had listened to a word I'd said.

I gritted my teeth. "Well, I, for one, am going to ask 'Mr Rossi' for his alibi."

40

Millie and Hannah waved me over to the long table booked by the project team as I walked into Giuseppe's pizza.

"Abigail, finally," Jeff exclaimed. "Decide what you want, all of us are set, and we're hungry."

I unwrapped my scarf and put my coat on the back of the chair while I tried to pay attention to what my body wanted, but that didn't help much, my body was giving me conflicting signals. Objectively, I was hungry, and the sensation intensified each time the kitchen door opened and delicious smells wafted through the main room, but I also had a heavy feeling in my stomach.

Marco, the devastatingly good-looking waiter, was going round the table, taking everybody's order at lightning speed.

When he got to me, I was still staring at the menu, reading the same line over and over again, but not really seeing the words. Everybody else had resumed their conversations, blissfully unaware of my internal turmoil. I shut my menu and, on autopilot, ordered my usual, pepperoni, artichokes' hearts, and mozzarella on a tomato sauce base.

Across the room, Frank was chatting with Sam, Nick, and Aaron as Giuseppe set their orders on the table. The gang, minus Elliott.

I was vaguely aware of the conversation at our table when Hannah tugged on my sleeve.

"Are they going to talk about work all night?"

"Not all night," I said, "but for a while."

Dinner with colleagues always started like a meeting, because, most of the time, work was the only thing we had in common. The gossip came later, once every open work topic had been wrapped up, and then, all bets were off.

I shivered as a gust of cold air drifted in from the door. Shruti and DC Robins had just walked in the restaurant. Interesting. Why were they here? I couldn't picture them as wanting to share a meal together, so it had to be because of the case. The question was, were they here because they had believed me after all, and they wanted to protect me, or were they here to protect Giuseppe *from* me?

I didn't realise I was staring at them until Hannah elbowed me. "Food's here."

And so it was.

Giuseppe and Marco were on the other side of the table, chatting with Anthony and Ram, aware that the project people would be bringing them regular business for months to come, but I wasn't paying attention to the conversation. All I could see was the strain and tiredness etched on Giuseppe's face.

Even if he had nothing to do with the murders, and if I'd completely misinterpreted the posts, hearts, and memes, and Elliott hadn't been his boyfriend, he still had known Elliott since they were teenagers.

I wanted to say something, but I knew it wasn't time yet. I wanted to wait until things were quieter, the restaurant emptier. If I was wrong—and given how bad a detective I'd been so far, that wasn't such a harebrained thought—I didn't want to stain Giuseppe's reputation.

Pizza was being eaten, drinks were being drunk, and all in all, the conversation was flowing reasonably well, when Giuseppe came back to our table.

"I need to leave early tonight," he said to no one in particular, "but don't worry, I left my assistant in the kitchen, he will be able to prepare any other dish you might want."

I checked my phone. It was barely eight, and Frank and the others were still eating. If he wasn't going out with his friends, what was going on?

My heart was beating hard in my chest, and for a brief moment, I feared my meal was going to come back out.

"Abigail?" Millie stared at me. "Are you alright?"

Forcing myself to breathe through my nose, I nodded. I wasn't okay, but I didn't want to worry her.

I looked over at Shruti's table, and her eyes were focused on Giuseppe. I searched her face for clues as to what she was thinking, but she was completely expressionless. DC Robins was eating with gusto, apparently unaware as to what was going on.

My body acted, and I was on my feet before I had a chance to realise what I was doing. "Giuseppe? Can I talk to you for a minute?" My voice had come out croaky. Not surprising, given that I really didn't want to have the conversation I was about to have.

"I'm sorry Abigail, but I really need to leave," he said.

No 'cara Abigail' for me tonight. It was as if he knew what I was going to ask.

"Please Giuseppe, it will only take a minute." I'd kept my voice down, but I could tell from the looks around the room that people had noticed there was something going on. Giuseppe had noticed too. And he had noticed Shruti and DC Robins two tables' away.

He indicated the small bar area with his chin. "Fine, let's go over there."

I gestured at Hannah, Millie, and the others at our table to remain seated, and followed him.

We stood side-by-side, facing away from the room, while I tried to work up the nerve to ask him.

He broke the silence. "You said you wanted to talk, but now you don't say anything? What's going on?"

There was no easy way to broach the subject, and as Hannah had told me before, I didn't do 'subtle'. What I did do well was 'blunt and direct'. I'd try it.

"Where were you the night Lynn James died, and the night Elliott died?"

The blood drained from Giuseppe's face and he froze for a second. "You don't wear gloves, do you? Why is this your business?"

"Please Giuseppe, I need to know."

He stared ahead for a few seconds, then sighed. "I was here, of course, I'm always here, you know this."

"Are you sure about this?"

I jumped out of my skin. Shruti was standing right behind us, and she'd obviously heard our conversation.

"Yes, of course I'm sure," Giuseppe said.

"Because we have asked your staff," she said, "and they said that you left them to do the closing, on both nights. They remembered, because they said it was unusual. They said that normally, *you* do the closing."

"Maybe I'd gone out with my friends, I don't remember," he said.

I remembered what Sam had said at the pub. "Not the night Lynn died. Your friends said you were working."

Sweat pearled on Giuseppe's forehead. "Maybe I'm

confused, I don't know. One of my oldest friends was killed, my mind . . . it's confused."

"Oldest friend," I said, "or boyfriend?"

"Boyfriend?!"

Some powers of observation I had, everybody was sneaking up on me. Behind me, Frank looked like he had been punched in the gut.

"You and Leo were dating?"

For a brief moment, I thought Giuseppe was going to fall apart, but the moment passed, and he pressed his lips tight together.

"Why would you think they were dating?" Frank asked me.

"If you look at Giuseppe's Facebook profile, a certain 'Leo' hearted most of his posts, and sent him cute memes. And on the other side, if you look at Elliott's company's page, Giuseppe liked and shared every single post going back at least two years."

"So? This doesn't prove anything. They were friends. We all were," Frank said.

"But did you have a secret girlfriend that you mentioned to no one, and did you make your mark on every single one of her social media posts?"

This time, Frank remained silent. Behind him, Millie and Hannah had crept up to our side of the room. Fair enough, they deserved to hear first-hand. I turned back to Giuseppe, whose arms were now crossed tight across his chest.

"What happened Giuseppe?"

He said nothing, and if it wasn't for his gaze shifting slightly down, I'd have thought he'd turned into a statue.

"Shall I tell you what I think happened?" Still no reaction, but Frank gave me a sign that he wanted to hear what I was thinking.

"I'm guessing Elliott was deep in the closet, though not so deep that he stayed well away from all things gay. His company mostly did corporate gigs, but he also did Pride events.

"You and Elliott somehow got together, probably while Lynn was working away. It would have been easy for him to cheat, she was away four nights a week.

"When Lynn started on this project, Elliott couldn't see you as much, or maybe even at all."

"Giuseppe?" Frank asked. "Say something. Tell her it's not true."

Giuseppe shook his head, lips still pressed tight. We all waited in silence, while the rest of the patrons carried on with their meals, unaware of the drama unfolding.

Giuseppe wiped his eyes and took a deep breath before speaking. "He wanted to break it off. Us. We'd been together for six years, we'd known each other for thirty. We were meant for each other."

Frank's face turned ashen. "Why didn't you say anything? I'm your friend too."

"Elliott didn't want to say anything. And we were happy. Until his wife started working in Winburyton. He said we couldn't be together anymore. It felt like he wanted to erase those years we were together. Like he wanted to erase *us*."

"Is that why you sent him the note?" Millie asked.

Giuseppe nodded. "He didn't reply to my texts, all my calls went straight to voicemail, he ignored my emails, he said he didn't want me to contact him again. How could he just throw us away like this?"

"You thought threatening him would change things?" I was feeling for him, but I couldn't understand how he could have thought that it had been a good idea.

Giuseppe wasn't holding back his tears anymore.

"You don't understand Abigail, I *wasn't* thinking, I was in pain."

We all remained quiet for a beat, hoping he would go on, but he only blew his nose.

"Nothing changed, right?" Millie asked.

Giuseppe shook his head 'no'.

"That's why you sent the second note? Was it a time and a place?"

"*Si*. He was avoiding me, so I asked him to meet me by the pond in the park, it's always empty there after the shops close."

"And then?" Now Shruti was chiming in? Now?

"I got there a little early, I was trying to make an effort, Elliott always complained that I was late everywhere. When *she* showed up, I didn't understand why she was there. She wasn't supposed to be there. She asked why I was threatening her, I tried to explain but she attacked me. We fought and . . ."

"And?" Jeff had joined us, and I could hear the pain in his voice. He wanted to know what had happened to a woman he'd cared a lot about.

"I don't know how it happened, I swear, but she was on the ground, and she wasn't moving, and I didn't know what to do."

"So you sent Elliott an email from her phone, pretending she'd gone to her mother's, and you pushed her in the pond?"

The nausea was back in full swing, and looking at the pain in Jeff's eyes, he felt the same.

I should have left Shruti get on with it, but I had to know "Why did you kill Elliott? If you loved him?"

"Yesterday afternoon, we met at my house, and we were back together, and it was like it was before, but he came to see me here at the end of the night, and he said he wanted to break up again. I tried to explain to him we could be together properly now, be seen out in public together, and . . ." Giuseppe's voice broke. "Elliott, he panicked. We were in the kitchen, and he took a knife. I tried to take it away from him, but he wouldn't let go." Tears streamed down his face. "Why wouldn't he let got?"

His last words had been barely audible through the crying and my heart broke for him.

We all stood silent for what felt like hours, dumbstruck. If this was what came from loving someone, I wasn't sure I wanted any part of it.

I wanted to undo it all. I wanted to not have asked Giuseppe to talk, I wanted for him to not have killed to people, I wanted for Lynn to not have asked me to help, I wanted for none of this to be my fault.

But I had gotten involved, and I had somehow un-covered the truth, and I felt dirty all over for it. If this was being a detective, I wanted no part of it. Why hadn't Arthur Conan Doyle explained? Sherlock Holmes never seemed to be fazed when he exposed murderers, he seemed, if not happy, at least satisfied, but I didn't, not even a little.

Shruti and DC Robins escorted Giuseppe outside and I just stared at them.

Millie put her hand on my shoulder.

"Abigail? Are you okay?"

"Not really."

"However much you liked Giuseppe, you still did a good thing."

Out of the corner of my eye, I saw Jeff, and the other consultants leave and get into taxis. Frank, Sam, and the other guys were gone too. It was just Hannah, Marco, Millie, and me in the restaurant. "I'm so sorry, Marco."

"Me too. But it's not your fault. He killed those people, you didn't."

Hannah tugged on my arm. "Come on, let's take you home."

41

Six days had passed since Millie had given me a deadline for asking her out on a date, and I had done nothing about it. A week ago, if I'd wanted to take a woman on a date, I would have taken her to Giuseppe's pizzeria, but Giuseppe's pizzeria had been closed since that night I confronted Giuseppe.

I checked my phone. Hannah had texted me back.

> Hannah: why don't you go to a bar for drinks
>
> Hannah: something low key no pressure and if youre bored you can get away quick

I did appreciate her attempts at helping, but it didn't help. I was almost certain I wouldn't want to escape a date with Millie, and I didn't want to take her someplace noisy where we couldn't talk. I packed my lunch and headed out the door. Maybe something would come to me during the day. I couldn't ask her out unless I had a plan.

At lunchtime, an idea had wormed its way into my brain and I headed for the car park. I drove into town, and parked as close to the shop as possible. The odds that Frank would say yes were tiny, but it was worth a shot.

I pushed the door. Frank seemed to have aged ten years since I'd last seen him.

"Abigail, my favourite customer."

"Hi Frank, how are you doing?"

"Hey, you know, it's not every day you find out your friend of thirty years murdered your other friend of thirty years that he'd been having a secret affair with."

"I am so sorry for your loss," I said. I was surprised to notice that I genuinely meant it.

"Thank you." Frank forced a smile on his face. "What can I get you?"

"A favour please."

Frank raised an eyebrow.

"Where are we going?" Millie asked

"It's a surprise," I said. "You put me in charge of this date, didn't you?"

"I did, but I'm curious."

"I think you'll like it, even if you find my company boring."

"You? Boring? Never," Millie teased.

I stopped in front of the shop. It was dark, much like all the other shops in the street. "We're here."

"Err, are you sure? This looks closed."

I smiled. "I'm sure." I leaned on the door and it opened. I took Millie's hand and pulled her in the shop after me.

"I know Frank, the cheesemonger and proprietor of this establishment pretty well, having been a loyal customer for well over a decade, and he's agreed to lend me his shop for our date."

I flipped the light switch Frank had told me about and cosy lighting turned on. He seemed to have strung fairy lights all over the place, and he'd put a tiny bistro table with two chairs in the space by the counter where clients would normally be queueing. The whole effect was magical.

"What do you think?" I asked anxiously.

"I . . . I'm not sure I understand," Millie said.

"We're having a private cheese tasting, paired with some amazing breads I got from Alice's earlier."

Millie's eyes glittered in the soft light. "We can try any cheese?"

"Any, and as much as you want."

Millie put her arms around my waist and pulled me in. Her lips grazed mine and she whispered, "Best date ever."

* * *

Dear Reader,

Did you enjoy reading this book? If so, I hope you'll take a moment to leave a review in order to let other readers know about it, even just one line can help!

Love, Sophie

PS: Sign-up to my newsletter at SophieMaddon.com and be the first to hear about *Two Sparks Of Mystery*, the second novel in the Abigail Palmer series!

Scan the code below for Goodreads reviews:

ACKNOWLEDGEMENTS

I always find it difficult to write acknowledgements, not because I'm not grateful, but because I always wonder whether I'm going too far, or whether I'm leaving some people out.

Do I thank Michael, for providing me a haven several weeks every year, giving me plenty of space to write, while making sure I'm well fed and get at least some exercise?

How about my American mum, who is always supportive and encouraging, even when I can tell she has her doubts about my latest ideas?

Marcus definitely should get thanks, for our Saturday morning walks, and letting me talk at him about plot points and any random questions that may happen to pop in my brain.

Eddie Louise too, for providing invaluable feedback on this novel (and on previous novels!). We may not talk often, but I value knowing you more than you can imagine.

David, for reading this manuscript and immediately talking to other ERP project people about it!

Gail, for providing inspiration for one of the characters in this novel.

My sister Claire, who doesn't get why I spend so much of my free time writing or thinking about writing, but who is always supportive nonetheless.

Last but definitely not least, my writing group—Bonetti, Nyx, Amber, Pikalee, Esther—I love the little time we get to spend together, you are all my people.

ALSO BY THIS AUTHOR

Young Adult

Your Knowledge Or Your Life?

Beyond the Threshold: A tale of Secrets and Shadows

Abigail Palmer Cozy Mystery Series

The Biscuit Factory Project:

A Slice of Mystery
Two Sparks of Mystery (coming soon)

ABOUT THE AUTHOR

Sophie Maddon is a neurodivergent author who has always been tagged at weird (but why be normal when you can be weird?) and universally acknowledged as a troublemaker.

She's currently living in the UK and is owned by a cat (half-panther if you ask the vet).

Subscribe to Sophie's newsletter!
Stay in touch: SophieMaddon.com